Five interesting things about Jessica Fox:

1. I can't resist stopping to look at newly married couples emerging from churches.

2. My palm-reader told me I have a lifeline that is shorter than my heart line. I assume this means I will be with my husband Rob in this life and the next. I just hope he will have learned to pick up his socks by then.

3. I have a phobia of elevators. On our honeymoon, the Eiffel Tower was definitely worth it. Until I realised I'd left my camera at the top.

4. I was once on a hen night where the groom appeared in the early hours and started chatting me up!

5. If my house was on fire, and I could only rescue one thing, it would be my antique tarot cards. Sorry, Rob.

The Hen Night Prophecies: The One that Got Away

Jessica Fox

little
black
dress

First published in 2009 by
LITTLE BLACK DRESS
An imprint of HEADLINE PUBLISHING GROUP

A LITTLE BLACK DRESS paperback

1

Cataloguing in Publication Data is available from the British Library

ISBN 978 0 7553 4957 9

Typeset in Transit511BT by Avon DataSet Ltd,
Bidford-on-Avon, Warwickshire

Printed and bound in Great Britain by
Clays Ltd, St Ives plc

Headline's policy is to use papers that are natural, renewable and
recyclable products and made from wood grown in sustainable forests.
The logging and manufacturing processes are expected to conform to the
environmental regulations of the country of origin.

HEADLINE PUBLISHING GROUP
An Hachette UK Company
338 Euston Road
London NW1 3BH

www.littleblackdressbooks.com
www.headline.co.uk
www.hachette.co.uk

Dedicated to Pat Farrell

Acknowledgements

With special thanks to Ruth Saberton

'Bollocks!'

Fern Moss stared in dismay at the car next to her. She'd been so busy craning her neck to see if the off licence was open she hadn't realised just how close she was to the shiny red paintwork. Parallel parking had never been her forte and her elderly Beetle was hardly equipped with state of the art power steering, so the first Fern knew about its fatal attraction to a Mercedes was a horrible scrunching sound.

'Oh no!'

As Fern stamped desperately on the brake her platform boot slipped on to the accelerator and with a sickening jolt her car became the proud owner of a third wing mirror, one which was considerably more expensive and electronically endowed than the others.

'Damn! Blast! Bugger!' Fern thumped her head against the steering wheel in despair. Bye-bye no claims bonus. Hello, irate Mercedes driver. Perhaps she should have checked her horoscope before she came out this year.

Fern's life truly was going from bad to worse. On top of everything, Seb had gone and he wasn't coming back. No. Correction. Seb had gone and Fern wasn't going to let him come back, no matter how sorry he said he was or how often he insisted Vanessa had meant nothing and that it was Fern he really loved. It was over. He could ring and text as much as he liked. She wasn't going to change her mind.

She killed the engine and took a deep breath. Her hurt feelings were red raw and every time she thought of Seb and Vanessa together it felt as though someone was dragging barbed wire through her guts. How could she ever get over such a betrayal? If she felt like howling every time she remembered they'd never again share a secret joke across the pub, that she'd never thread her fingers through his silky black hair or curl up with him at night, it didn't mean she should cave in and forgive him, did it?

No, it bloody well didn't.

Sighing, Fern opened the glove box, sweeping

magazines, unravelling cassettes and Tampax on to the floor, and bingo! There was her emergency chocolate supply.

Unwrapping a bar of Dairy Milk and biting off a chunk, Fern munched gratefully. If ever a girl deserved a few thousand calories it was now. After all, wasn't chocolate supposed to be a love substitute? In many ways it was far superior. Chocolate never dropped its socks on the floor or left the loo seat up so that you fell down the bowl in the middle of the night. And chocolate certainly never cheated on you with a blonde Twiglet woman from its office. With chocolate a girl knew exactly where she stood.

Fern had never quite known where she stood with Seb, which had been exciting and frustrating in equal measure. His job as an advertising creative at one of London's leading agencies had been glamorous and she'd certainly enjoyed the novelty of attending functions at hotel bars and fancy restaurants. Life with Seb, a charismatic charmer with classic dark good looks, had never been straightforward but it had been fun. Their arguments had been legendary; both being creative types Fern supposed that they'd been bound to clash, but the making up had more than compensated.

Fern wasn't going to think about all that right now, though, not when she was on her way to her best friend's hen night. Tonight was about celebrating Zoe and Steve's relationship rather than dwelling on the car crash of her own.

And talking about car crashes, maybe she ought to think about sorting out the damage she'd just done to the Mercedes.

Tearing up a stray magazine and retrieving an eyebrow pencil from the assorted clutter on the dashboard Fern wrote out her name and phone number, telling herself that a lesser (but richer) person would have just driven away. But Fern, with her finely developed Catholic sense of guilt, couldn't live with such shoddy behaviour.

She'd get to heaven yet.

Clambering out of her Beetle, she tucked the note under the Mercedes' windscreen wiper and prayed the owner wouldn't return just yet. Call her a chicken but she'd rather be a safe distance away when he discovered what she'd done. Like maybe the other side of London.

She shrugged her big beaded bag on to her shoulder and darted across the road to the off licence, dodging the rush hour traffic and trying her hardest to claw back some time by running, which was easier said than done in four-inch platform boots. Glancing at her watch, she groaned. She was really late now, which wasn't that unusual since she was famous for her inability to be anywhere on time. Fern never meant to be late – in fact she always had every intention of arriving early – but things had a habit of happening and delaying her. It was like an unwritten law of physics or something. Take this evening, for instance. Just as Fern had been about to leave the Angel Theatre, sitting back on her heels admiring the effect of the set she was working on, the wardrobe mistress had invited her to have a rummage in the props cupboard. One tiara, a set of fairy wings and a green velvet cloak later Fern was well and truly behind schedule. Hence the frantic dash through the Friday evening traffic while attempting to reapply her make-up every time she met a red light, and her even worse than usual parking skills.

She'd buy a really nice bottle of champagne to make up for being late, Fern decided as she clomped through the off licence, pausing to admire the bottles of Cristal and Dom Pérignon before moving on to the Moët. She'd just been paid so maybe she'd buy two bottles to make the evening go with a swing? Zoe had said that there'd be five of them at her house for a quiet girls' night in. No strippers, she'd said firmly, fixing Fern with a beady look, and certainly no stretch limos and dancing on tables in clubs. They'd get a takeaway and maybe watch a DVD. She wanted a civilised gathering not a raucous party.

It was all a bit disappointing really, Fern decided as she selected two bottles of champagne and meandered to the till. A hen night was the perfect excuse to let your hair down, something Zoe hadn't done for ages. It wasn't so long ago that Zoe had been the original wild child, but nowadays she and Steve were more of an old married couple than Richard and Judy. It would have been fun to have a really wild night out. They could have dressed up and hit a club, maybe even had a theme . . .

'Fancy dress?' the shopkeeper asked.

'Sorry?' Dragging her thoughts back to the present Fern smiled at the elderly man behind the counter.

'Your clothes.' He nodded at her outfit. 'Going to a party?'

'Oh!' Fern's small silver-ringed fingers flew to her mouth as she caught sight of her reflection in the glass of a refrigerator. A small figure stared back at her, blue eyes wide, a tiara perched on top of her blond curls. A long green cloak and glittery fairy wings teamed with crimson flares and platform boots completed the look.

'Suits you,' he continued, ringing up the purchases. 'A seventies party, is it?'

'It's my best friend's hen night,' said Fern, deciding against telling him the shoes and flares were actually her own clothes. How could she have forgotten she was wearing half the props cupboard? Her memory was a Swiss cheese lately, filled with hideous thoughts about Seb and Vanessa one moment and the next consumed with the colours and intricacies of her latest set design. Cheeks ketchup-red, Fern pulled the tiara off. She really had to get a grip.

'That's forty pounds,' said the man, lovingly wrapping each bottle in tissue paper. 'Do you want a carrier?'

'Please.' Fern delved into her bag for her purse which always lurked in the deepest depths, among the remnants of tissues and leaky biros. Seb had liked to joke that Fern owned the world's first Tardis bag and maybe Lord Lucan and Shergar were in there too. The bag was so big that sometimes Fern rummaged for ages before locating her keys or her purse. Today was one such occasion.

'Sorry,' she said, taking the bag off her shoulder and peering into it. 'I know my purse is in here somewhere.'

At least she hoped it was, but several minutes' more rummaging proved fruitless. God, surely she hadn't lost her purse again? It had to be in there, didn't it? Unfortunately, though, more frantic rummaging followed by a hasty tipping out of the entire contents on to the counter revealed that the purse was missing. Aghast, Fern stared at the mountain of debris. Oyster card, mobile, spare socks, cigarettes, a battered Jilly Cooper, theatre tickets to the production of *A Midsummer Night's Dream* she'd designed the set for, and maybe even a kitchen sink, but certainly no purse.

How hideously embarrassing.

'It's not here,' she whispered.

'Doesn't seem to be,' the shopkeeper agreed. 'Still, don't panic, my dear. These things have a habit of turning up. Where did you see it last?'

Fern racked her brains. Then it came to her. 'I was on eBay last night! I must have left it by the computer! Phew!'

'There you are then. Have you got a credit card?'

'Not on me. What a pain. I'll have to put the champagne back.'

'You can't possibly have a hen night without champagne,' the man said. Peering over his glasses at the heaped contents of Fern's bag he plucked out the theatre tickets and studied them thoughtfully. 'How about I take these in return for the champagne?'

'Really?' Hope fizzed through Fern like the bubbles in the Moët. 'Are you sure?'

'Absolutely. The reviews in the *Guardian* were marvellous and my wife will be delighted. That's if you're happy to exchange them? These tickets are probably worth more than the champagne. In fact, take another bottle. I insist.'

'That's brilliant! Thank you,' Fern cried. To be honest she hadn't intended to use the tickets anyway. While creating the set she'd watched so many rehearsals of the *Dream* she could pretty much perform it solo. And besides, it was hard to feel the same about the fairies when you'd seen them all crowded round the stage door smoking and knew that Puck was sleeping with Titania. But swapping the tickets for Moët? That was her idea of magic!

This was going to be a great hen night!

2

That, Fern thought, parking much more carefully this time between two shiny four by fours, was the journey from hell.

How was it possible for a fifteen-mile journey to take over an hour? It was just ridiculous! And where did people in Hampstead park? Locking the car door and pushing her blond curls behind her ears she decided she had no choice but to jog the three streets to Zoe's house, otherwise she'd be even later.

I really must get fit, thought Fern as she pounded along the pavement, the fairy wings boinging in time with each stride. Maybe she should invest in a pair of trainers and a gym membership. Nobody of thirty-one should pant and gasp this much after sprinting only a few yards. Perhaps she'd ask Libby, Zoe's ultra-fit and sporty sister, for some tips, although she already had a sneaking suspicion what Libby would say. Probably something along the lines of giving up the chocolate, booze and sneaky cigarettes, three of Fern's favourite things in life.

Maybe she'd just walk instead.

Slowing her pace and clutching at a stitch Fern hobbled the rest of the way, and paused on the doorstep to get her breath back. Then she straightened her wings, smoothed some damp curls back from her flushed cheeks and lifted the heavy brass door knocker. Time to party!

'Thank God!' cried Zoe, flinging open the smart blue door, and pulling Fern in for a hug. 'We were about to send out a search and rescue team!'

'Sorry,' puffed Fern, 'but you'll never believe what happened to me on the way over.'

'Wouldn't I?' Zoe arched a beautifully waxed eyebrow, and scanned her best friend affectionately. 'What was it this time? Lost car keys? Running out of petrol? Hang on! I've got it! Aliens?'

Fern flushed. A while back she'd mistaken the landing lights of a 747 for flying saucers, an easy mistake to make after watching *ET* and polishing off the dregs of the Blossom Hill. The bigger mistake had been telling her friends, who would never let her live it down.

'Very funny.'

'Sorry, hon, but you are such a drama queen.' Grabbing her friend's hand warmly in hers, Zoe led Fern into the hallway, all polished oak floors and black and white shots from a selection of the costume dramas she'd produced. 'I didn't mean to tease. What really happened?'

'I pranged the Beetle. Nothing major but I managed to knock a wing mirror off a Mercedes when I was parking.'

'Oh, Fern! That's rotten luck.'

Fern shrugged. 'It was my rubbish driving more than bad luck. Then when I was in the off licence I realised I'd lost my purse.'

Zoe rolled her hazel eyes. 'Not the dreaded purse again? We need to superglue it to you!'

Fern laughed. 'That's one solution, I suppose! Anyway, never mind my traumas. We need to celebrate your final weekend of freedom.'

'I'm up for that.' Zoe took Fern's velvet cloak, not batting an eyelid at the fairy wings and flares – she'd seen Fern in far odder attire over the years since they'd been friends. 'I just hope the boys look after Steve tonight and don't handcuff him naked to a lamppost or do something awful like putting him on a ferry. That's why he's having his stag night now rather than just before the wedding. I haven't spent the last year arranging our special day to have it all wrecked at the eleventh hour. I've worked really hard to get everything right.'

This was possibly the understatement of the year. Zoe had lived and breathed her wedding for months. Every detail had been meticulously planned with the same determination that had enabled her to become one of the BBC's youngest and most successful scriptwriters. Not that Fern had been surprised. Everything Zoe did was thoroughly planned and perfectly executed, so why should her wedding be any different?

'It'll be fine,' Fern soothed. 'He's only having a meal with some of his colleagues. Stop worrying and enjoy your night. I've bought us some champagne.'

'Thanks, hon! Let's pop it in the fridge to chill for a bit. The others are all in the kitchen anyway. Priya brought some nibbles with her and we've all been tucking in. Come on through.'

Fern followed Zoe through to her amazing kitchen. Steve and Zoe might have been about to get married but this was no starter home. With Zoe adapting period dramas that were sold worldwide, and Steve also riding high in the BBC, they'd been able to totally indulge themselves when they'd bought and refurbished the house. Zoe was the kind of domestic goddess who made Nigella look amateurish, and when it came to designing the kitchen she'd really surpassed herself. Fern's entire flat could have fitted in it with room to spare. With a gleaming glass roof, Delabole slate floor and a range that looked like a lost part of the Starship Enterprise, the kitchen was simply stunning. Two squashy leather sofas and a giant plasma screen made it the perfect space for chilling with a glass of wine, or chatting over one of Zoe's fantastic meals.

This evening three women were seated at the glass table, sipping drinks and talking away nineteen to the dozen. Fern knew two of them, although not particularly well, since they'd only met through Zoe. The pretty Asian girl with the razor-sharp bob was Priya, and sloshing wine into her glass was Zoe's Amazonian sister Libby, all long limbs and mischievous grin. Fern didn't recognise the refined redhead working her way through a bowl of nachos.

'Hi, Fern,' grinned Libby, waving her wine glass in the air. 'You've got some catching up to do!'

'Do you know everyone?' said Zoe, flinging the Moët into the fridge and pulling out a bottle of Chardonnay. 'That's my drunken sister hogging the booze and next to her is Priya who did that documentary on the set of *Jane Eyre*.'

'I loved that bedroom set you did for the scene between Jane and Rochester.' Priya smiled at Fern, fanning her face with a slender hand. 'The four-poster with the red drapes was so sexy!'

Fern flushed with pleasure. 'Thanks. I had a lot of fun designing it.'

'Not as much fun as Rochester and Jane had trying it out,' said Priya.

Fern plopped herself down at the table and sighed with relief at taking her weight off her platformed feet. It had been a long tough day and now she could get steadily sloshed with the girls. Bliss.

'I'm Charlotte,' said the redhead, looking up from her nachos. 'Steve's sister.'

'Soon to be my sister-in-law!' Handing Fern a glass, Zoe sat next to Charlotte and smiled. 'How crazy is that? In just over a week's time we'll be related.'

Charlotte pulled a face. 'What's crazy is that anyone wants to get married at all. You must be mad. Don't say I didn't warn you.'

The atmosphere was suddenly so thick that you could have knitted it. Fern recalled Zoe once mentioning that Steve's sister had been through a pretty nasty divorce. Talk about the spectre at the feast.

'You know me, I never listen to anyone,' said Zoe so airily that Fern realised she'd had this conversation many times already. 'I'll give marriage a chance.'

'So would I if it was to Steve,' Fern agreed quickly. 'You were so lucky to have him as your mentor when you joined the Beeb.'

Zoe's eyes grew dreamy. 'Mmm, wasn't I?'

From the minute Steve first laid eyes on Zoe he'd been smitten, and luckily for him his mentee had felt the same way.

'You two are perfect together.' Priya sighed.

'Pass the sick bucket,' muttered Charlotte.

'We're supposed to be celebrating Steve and Zoe's wedding,' Libby reminded her sharply. 'This is a happy occasion.'

'Sorry.' Charlotte's hyacinth-blue eyes filled. 'Just ignore me. If there's one man who's an exception to the rule that all the rest are bastards then it's my brother.'

'If Steve was a good Hindu boy I'd fight you for him,' Priya joked.

'And if you weren't my sister I'd make a play for him myself!' giggled Libby.

Zoe laughed. 'Hands off. He's taken.'

'Seriously,' Charlotte said, 'I know you two will be really happy. If I didn't love you both so much I'd probably be consumed with jealousy.'

It was time to derail this melancholy conversation, Fern decided. Raising her glass, she said, 'How about a toast? To Zoe and Steve. The happiest couple I know!'

'Zoe and Steve,' chorused the girls, chinking their glasses, while Zoe blushed milkshake-pink.

Several more toasts and many more glasses of wine later even Charlotte was in the party mood. Fern's Moët was cracked open while more crisps and a gorgeous homemade guacamole dip appeared as though by magic. After another round of drinks Zoe was wearing Fern's tiara, a net curtain as a veil and an L-plate that Libby had pinned on to her back.

'Now it feels like a proper hen night!' said Fern, stepping back and admiring their handiwork.

'That reminds me, I've got you a present.' Priya fished a beautifully wrapped gift out of her bag and handed it to Zoe. 'Something for your wedding night.'

'Lingerie?' Zoe wondered, shaking the box.

'I wouldn't do that,' said Priya. 'It might—'

Buzz buzz buzz, went the box. All the girls leapt back, apart from Priya, who chuckled.

Buzz buzz.

'Is this what I think it is?' asked Zoe.

'I don't know. Open it and find out.'

'Knowing my luck it's a giant hornet,' Zoe groaned as she untied the ribbon and pulled off the lid. 'Oh my God! I wish it was!'

'It's giant all right,' gasped Libby.

On the table buzzing away with a life all of its own was the most enormous vibrator Fern had ever seen, not that she'd seen that many. This terrifying specimen was ten inches of black plastic complete with realistic veins (why?) and what looked like revolving spikes. The girls stared at it in fascinated horror.

'Oh my God!' breathed Fern, watching the thing sway and buzz. 'That's not a vibrator, it's a weapon of mass destruction. My eyes are watering just thinking about it!'

'I think that's the point,' shrieked Priya and they all collapsed into fits of giggles.

'Shush!' Dashing tears from her eyes Zoe held her hand up. 'I think I heard the door. Listen!'

Sure enough the loud thud of the brass knocker reverberated through the kitchen. Libby leapt to her feet. 'That'll be my present, babes!'

Zoe buried her face in her hands. 'Oh, God, Libs. You didn't get me a stripper?'

'Of course not! How clichéd would that be? I've booked something far more exciting than a mere stripper!' Pausing for emphasis, Libby looked round at the four expectant women and her eyes sparkled with excitement. 'Girls, prepare to meet our very own fortune-teller!'

3

'A fortune-teller? Has my sister flipped?' asked Zoe as Libby raced off to answer the door.

'I've never had my cards read,' said Fern thoughtfully. 'It could be fun.'

Charlotte frowned. 'What if she tells you something terrible?'

'Of course she won't. It's all nonsense,' Priya scoffed. 'It's impossible to tell the future. Although it would be really useful to know what was coming so that you could organise things better.'

But Fern wasn't so certain. She'd lost count of the times she'd scared herself silly watching *Most Haunted*. Enough people believed in mediums to suggest there was something in it. Maybe the fortune-teller would be able to shed some light on her ill-fated relationship with Seb. At this thought a knot of excitement tightened in her stomach. She couldn't help thinking it would have been very handy to have known Seb was a cheating scumbag *before* she'd got involved with him.

'Maybe it's better to be forewarned?'

'You have a point there,' Charlotte agreed, sloshing more wine into her glass. 'God, I wish I were psychic. I'd never have got married and I'd have saved myself a fortune in solicitor's bills.'

'But there must have been good things about your marriage. It couldn't all have been bad,' Zoe protested. 'If you'd been warned not to do it you'd have missed so many experiences. Surely life's about learning and growing?'

Charlotte pulled a face. 'That's easy to say if you've never been through a divorce. No, I'll take all the cosmic input going. In fact, let me go first!'

Zoe laughed. 'Be my guest!'

'Everyone, this is Angela, our fortune-teller!' cried Libby, bursting into the kitchen.

Fern wasn't sure quite what she'd expected a fortune-teller to look like. All long floating gypsy skirts, hooped earrings and headscarves, she supposed, like something out of *Carmen*; or maybe dressed from head to toe in midnight black with a crystal ball in one hand and tarot cards in the other, muttering to her spirit guide. What she hadn't expected was somebody as ordinary looking as this woman who was smiling and saying hello. She looked just like someone's mum rather than Mystic Meg. With her cuddly frame, rosy cheeks, greying curls and M&S slacks she was about as exotic as a trip to Margate and Fern was surprised to feel a stab of disappointment. She hadn't realised just how much she'd been hoping that she might learn something about her future. How ridiculous, she told herself sternly. You know it's all rubbish.

'Angela, thanks for coming.' Ever the gracious hostess, Zoe rose to her feet and kissed her unexpected guest on the cheek. 'Can I get you a drink? Wine? Champagne?'

'Oh, no thanks, love, I don't drink when I'm working.' Depositing her bag on the worktop Angela beamed at the gathered girls. 'But I wouldn't say no to a nice cup of tea.'

'Is that so you can read the leaves?' Fern asked hopefully.

'Bless you, no! Who reads tea leaves nowadays? It's all tea bags or fancy coffee. I'm just partial to a nice brew. I'll have two sugars though; these readings take a lot of energy!'

'I'll get you settled while Zoe makes the tea,' suggested Libby. 'I thought we'd use the conservatory, if that's all right? It's more private in there.'

'That's fine,' Zoe said, filling the kettle with filtered water. 'We'll work out who's going first and they can bring the tea in.'

While Libby settled Angela in the girls bickered good-naturedly about who should have the first reading. Eventually they decided that as the bride to be Zoe should go first, followed by Priya, who was the most sceptical, then Charlotte, then Libby and finally Fern. Topping up their drinks and leaving Zoe to slip through the red velvet curtain and into the conservatory, the girls moved into the sitting room to give her more privacy. While Libby put on Wham! and dragged Priya to her feet for a dance, Fern sank into a chair, nursing her drink.

Perhaps Angela would be able to tell her who her perfect man really was. It might save a lot of hassle in the long run if she knew exactly who to look out for. Most girls kissed a lot of frogs before they found their prince but Fern's princes had a nasty habit of turning into toads. It was all very annoying.

A little while later Zoe stumbled into the sitting room and the girls clamoured to know what Angela had said. Annoyingly, Zoe was in no rush to give anything away, but as she poured a glass of wine her hands shook so much that the straw-yellow liquid spilled all over the table.

'What's up?' Libby asked. 'Did she get it all wrong?'

Zoe shook her glossy head. 'No. She was spookily accurate about most things. I've never known anything like it. She knew things I've never told anyone.'

Charlotte squeezed her shoulder. 'Don't look so worried, Zo. It's probably lucky guesses and generic stuff. It's your hen night, after all, so it wouldn't take a lot to guess that relationships and marriage are on the cards.'

'Is that what she talked about? Marriage?' asked Fern.

'I'd rather not discuss it yet.' Zoe reached for her drink and took a big gulp. 'Why don't we keep our readings to ourselves for now and compare them later?'

The girls agreed, feeling slightly disappointed but not wanting to press the issue and spoil Zoe's night. One by one each took her turn to have a reading and returned just as dazed and perplexed as the bride to be. Whatever Angela was saying, Fern thought nervously, it was certainly having an effect on them.

'Your turn, Fern,' Libby told her, rejoining the group after her reading and looking thoughtful.

'Do I really want to?' Anticipation was making Fern's skin prickle. 'You lot all look traumatised.'

'Well, she could have been worse,' said Charlotte. 'She knew all about my divorce and she's never met me before!'

It was on the tip of Fern's tongue to point out that she didn't know Charlotte either and also knew all about her divorce but she stopped herself just in time. It was Zoe's hen night and she'd agreed to go along with this. It was only a bit of fun, after all.

With a sigh, she abandoned her wine and walked through the house to the conservatory. Above the glass kitchen roof a molasses-black sky was peppered with stars and the darkness seemed to press against the windows. She pushed aside the heavy red curtain and saw Angela seated on a Lloyd Loom armchair behind a coffee table which she'd covered with a beautiful silk cloth. The table lamp threw a pool of buttery light across a deck of tarot cards.

'Hello, love.' Angela gave her a warm smile. 'Last but not least, eh? Sit yourself down and let's make a start, shall we?'

Fern obeyed, glad to take a seat because her legs

had suddenly turned to overcooked spaghetti. In the shadowy atmosphere Angela no longer felt like someone's mum and Fern's mouth dried as though she'd swallowed half the Sahara.

'You've been unlucky in love for one so young,' murmured Angela, gently picking up Fern's right hand and tracing the lines on it with her forefinger. 'You've made some bad decisions, chosen some unsuitable people.'

Fern laughed nervously. 'You're sounding as though I regularly date men who make Adolf Hitler look like the Tooth Fairy.'

But Angela wasn't laughing. 'Someone's betrayed you in the worst possible way. He's hurt you badly and you're wondering whether it's your fault, but it isn't. He's made a big mistake, darling, and he knows that.'

Okay, don't panic, Fern told herself, it's just a lucky guess. Maybe one of the others mentioned me in their reading?

'He's one less tie for you to worry about,' Angela continued, 'and maybe he's done you a favour, because you're at a bit of a crossroads with your career, aren't you?'

'Mmm.' Actually this was true. Her friend Alek had recently set up a satellite company in Prague and was really keen for her to work for him. Fern was seriously tempted but reluctant to leave her friends and family. Still, it was all pretty generic stuff. She was in her early thirties and bound to be thinking about careers and relationships. Angela was just making some lucky generalisations.

'You'll turn a corner, though, darling. It will all become clear. Don't be afraid to make a change. There's some very powerful stuff coming through for you. It's all good and you'll recognise it when it arrives.' Angela pushed the tarot cards towards Fern. 'Give these a shuffle and then cut the deck.'

Fern did as she was told.

Leaning forward, Angela turned over the first card. 'Oh! The Tower!'

Fern looked and wished she hadn't bothered. The card showed lots of unhappy people falling off a crumbling castle into lots of very orange flames. It made a cruise on the *Titanic* look like a jolly day out.

'This is the past, darling. Chaos, despair and change.'

'Sounds about right,' sighed Fern.

'I'm seeing a man.' Although Angela was staring at the card her eyes were blank and focused on some faraway spot. Fern felt goose bumps Mexican wave across her arms. 'He's holding his chest, his heart region, my darling, is that right? He's telling me that you mustn't feel responsible for his passing. It was his time to go and he doesn't blame you at all. Does that make sense?'

Fern's chin nearly hit the table.

'I'm getting the name Roger,' Angela said slowly. 'He's showing me the colour pink and pointing at his nose. Does that mean something to you?'

Fern's blood seemed to grow thick in her veins and the hairs on her scalp prickled. 'Roger was my dad,' she whispered. 'He had a heart attack.'

How had Angela managed to pick up details so private that she hadn't even shared them with Zoe? Nobody outside her family knew any of this. It wasn't a part of her life that she was proud of.

'It was sudden,' Angela told her. 'Roger says he didn't feel a thing. He's so sorry for shouting at you. He wants you to know that he loves you very much.'

Fern's eyes filled with tears and for a split second she was back in 1991, a stroppy argumentative teenager rowing with her father about her new nose stud and the pink stripes that she'd dyed into her hair. He'd ordered her to take the stud out and sort out the hair and Fern had yelled at him to go to hell. The row escalated until suddenly Roger had clutched at his chest and crashed on to the floor.

Minutes later he was dead. It didn't matter that nobody had known he'd had heart problems or that his business was in trouble: Fern had blamed herself for years. Even though she knew deep down she'd just been a typical adolescent she still felt a horrible sense of guilt.

'He says he doesn't blame you, darling. He wants you to be happy.'

There was a football in Fern's throat. She dug her nails into the palms of her hands. She wasn't going to let the tears roll. If she did she didn't think they'd ever stop.

'He likes your hair better now, darling. He says he didn't mean to go to such extreme lengths to make you change it, though! And who was the man with the make-up? He didn't like him, did he?'

Fern was lost for words. She'd been crazy about Boy George but her father had loathed the make-up-wearing musician. He'd teased her relentlessly about him. All this was hitting just a bit too close to home. There was no way Angela could have known such personal details.

Maybe there really was something in this psychic business.

Feeling uncomfortable and more than a little bit unnerved, Fern decided it was time to put this stuff to the test. She'd ask Angela a standard question and of course she'd get a pat answer in return, an answer that she and the girls could laugh about later on.

'When will I meet the one?' she blurted. 'Never mind my past or anything else. When am I going to meet my soulmate?'

Angela regarded Fern sadly. 'You already had him, my love, and you let him go.'

Fern stared at her in disbelief. 'Let him go?'

'You've met your other half already, darling, but you were too blind to see it. You didn't recognise him for who he really was, did you?'

'Obviously not.' Fern was horrified. She was thirty-one, most of her friends were coupled up and all the single men she knew were single for a very good reason. Could she have screwed up her one chance of happiness?

'Is he one of my exes?' Already Fern was running through the roll-call of shame. Whom had she stupidly let go?

'I can't see any more, love. I'm sorry. Maybe we should finish the reading now?'

As she stumbled out of the conservatory Fern's thoughts were whirling faster than her washing machine on spin cycle. Who was her soulmate? Whom had she overlooked?

Back in the sitting room Mika was blaring out from the CD player. The contrast between the seriousness of the conservatory and the lively music was very disorientating.

'Well?' Libby demanded. 'What did she tell you? Nobody else will say a word and I'm starting to think I've wasted my money. Maybe I should have got a stripper after all.'

'Are you all right, Fern?' Charlotte asked. 'You look very pale.'

'I'm fine,' Fern fibbed. 'But it was a bit intense.'

Libby sighed. 'I'll see Angela out and try to pretend we've had a good time. Next time I have a good idea just hit me over the head with a mallet or something.'

Casting a quick glance across the room Fern noticed that everyone else was looking really awkward. Perhaps it wasn't just Fern who'd had an uncomfortably accurate reading? Zoe especially appeared lost in thought and Priya was steadily gnawing her nails. She'd be up to her elbows soon unless Fern took matters into her own hands. Literally!

Lifting a tray of sambucas that Zoe had just poured, she started to waltz around the room with the drinks held high above her head. It was a dangerous balancing act and keeping in time with the music was really tricky, but at least everyone's attention was on Fern rather than the strange experiences of the evening. Soon they were all laughing at her antics.

'Come on, you lot,' she panted as she shimmied round the sitting room. 'Get off those sofas and on to the dance floor if you want a sambuca! From now on the only spirits we're interested in come in bottles!'

But even as she handed out the drinks and moved to the cheerful music Fern knew that this wasn't exactly true. There was only one thought on her mind now and unless she answered it soon she'd go crackers.

If she'd already met the one then who on earth was he?

And, even more important, how could she find out?

'One skinny latte and a cheese and ham panini as requested.' Zoe deposited the spoils of her trip to the café on the table and fixed Fern with a stern look. 'Now eat something, for goodness' sake, babes. You look terrible.'

'Thanks for pointing that out,' Fern said, thinking that it was hardly surprising she looked terrible when she was feeling as though a group of break dancers were getting on down in her skull, 'but I think it may take slightly more than carbs to sort me out. Maybe a bucketful of Resolve and a darkened room might be more appropriate?'

Zoe laughed. 'I may stretch to Nurofen but not until you've eaten. Now stop moaning and tuck in!'

It was Saturday lunchtime and the girls were sitting outside by the Thames, watching the glittering water as it flowed past and enjoying the warmth of the spring sunshine on their faces. Or rather Zoe was enjoying the sunshine while Fern winced and screwed up her eyes against the light.

'Can't someone turn the sun down?' she wailed, trying to shade her eyes with her hands. 'Or maybe we could we sit inside?'

'Exactly how much sambuca did you drink last night?' Zoe wondered, fishing in her Marc Jacobs bag for a pair of sunglasses and handing them to Fern.

'Too much,' Fern groaned as she put them on. 'I'm never drinking again!'

'I've heard that before!' Zoe laughed. 'In fact I think I heard that every Saturday morning for the whole of the three years we were at uni.'

'I mean it this time. If I never drink sambuca again it'll be too soon.'

'Strangely enough, you're not the only one to have expressed that sentiment. Libby and Charlotte both looked a bit green around the gills when they left.'

Fern smiled. After she'd given the sambucas out the drinking had begun in earnest, which would explain why Priya was still crashed out in Zoe's spare room and Libby had been practically mainlining Resolve before she'd left. It was just as well Steve was still away on his stag weekend, because his fiancée and her friends looked far from a pretty sight this morning.

'It was a good evening, though, wasn't it?' Fern asked cautiously. She didn't want to mention Angela's prophecy first but it was playing on her mind. She wondered if Zoe felt the same way.

'It was a fantastic night. There's nothing I like more than spending time with my best girls,' Zoe agreed. 'I could have done without the fortune-telling part though. I'm not really into that kind of thing, to be honest. Still, the others seemed to think she was really accurate. Even Charlotte was impressed, which takes some doing!'

'Did you think she was good?'

'She certainly knew a lot of things that were very personal to me,' Zoe replied thoughtfully. 'What about your reading? Did she say anything that made sense to you?'

Fern spooned some froth from her latte and took a sip. Caffeine shot into her bloodstream and instantly she started to feel more human. In fairness, she wasn't so much hungover as exhausted. Once the party had finished she had tossed and turned on Zoe's futon, alcohol and memories of Angela's reading mingling in a really unpleasant way. When she'd finally drifted off her sleep was uneasy and haunted by Angela's words which seemed to be stuck on repeat, echoing round and around her dreams until she'd woken with a dry mouth and a pounding heart. After that she'd lain awake and watched the sweep of headlights across the ceiling while running through a mental list of her exes, desperately trying to work out which one she'd let go. But even when the cool light of dawn trickled through the chink in the curtains she was none the wiser. As far as she could see all her exes were exes for very good reasons. Weren't they?

'Are you okay, babes?' Zoe's eyes were hazel circles of concern. 'You look really worried. What did she say to you?'

Fern sighed and put her coffee cup down with a clatter. Her hands were trembling, though whether from too much alcohol or from the shock of Angela's knowing things that were totally private she couldn't tell.

'Hey!' Zoe's cool slim fingers rested on hers. 'What's up?'

'She knew all about my dad,' Fern said quietly. 'She told me how he died.'

Zoe raised a groomed pre-wedding eyebrow. 'That could have been guesswork, babes. What is it they call it? Cold reading?'

Fern shook her head. 'No way. It was far too accurate for that. She knew really personal stuff, things I've never told anyone outside the family. She couldn't possibly have made it up. She was spot on.'

'So she's the real deal?'

'I think she must be,' said Fern. Then she noticed that beneath her St Tropez tan Zoe had paled. 'What did she say to you?'

'Never mind me right now,' Zoe said quickly. 'Mine was all boring stuff in comparison. What else did she say? And don't try to pretend there's nothing more, Fern Moss, because I know you and I know when you're upset.'

'You promise you won't laugh or think I'm being stupid?'

'Of course I won't!'

Fern took a deep breath. 'I know I'm supposed to think that women don't need men to complete them and all that stuff but I asked Angela when I'd find my soulmate.' She blushed. 'How clichéd is that?'

'Everyone wants to be loved, babes.' Zoe squeezed her hand. 'Besides, I'm hardly likely to give you a lecture, am I? Not after being the ultimate Bridezilla for the last six months! So, what did Angela tell you? Who is he?'

'Well, apparently that's the million-dollar

question. She told me I've already found him but I let him go.' Even as she repeated the psychic's words Fern's stomach gave a horrible lurch of fear. How could she have been so careless?

'The one that got away,' Zoe breathed. 'That's so romantic!'

'Is it?' Fern didn't think it sounded romantic at all. As far as she was concerned it was a great big pain in the butt and hideously complicated to boot. Not only was she going to have to figure out which of her exes was her soulmate, she was going to have to do some serious grovelling and eat an enormous slice of humble pie.

She was getting indigestion just thinking about it.

Zoe was rummaging in her bag. As Fern watched she pulled out a pen and her beautiful leather-bound Smythson's notebook which had the words *Wedding Plans* etched across it in gold italic leaf. Turning to the back she selected a new creamy page and flourished the pen. 'We need a plan of action!'

Fern rolled her eyes. Zoe took planning ahead to the extreme. At uni she'd always met deadlines while Fern had overdosed on Pro Plus and stayed up all night in order to complete an entire term's worth of essays.

'Don't look at me like that!' Zoe scolded, pen

poised over the page. 'Right then, let's get our thinking caps on. Who do you think he *could* be? Is there anyone who springs to mind?'

Fern gulped down some more coffee and thought hard. As she'd lain in bed last night images from the past had spooled before her vision like a home movie. Ultimately there were only three men that she could truly say she'd been in love with.

The first memory came with a bittersweet flood of nostalgia. After all, there's no love like first love.

Luke Scottman had been her first serious boyfriend and they'd been together for most of their time at university. She and Zoe had met him through the drama society when they'd all appeared in *A Midsummer Night's Dream*. Fern had hardly believed her luck when she was cast as Hermia opposite the tall, good-looking northerner with the piercing denim blue eyes who'd been picked for Lysander. Pretending to be in love with him had to have been one of the easiest acting jobs in history and pretty soon life had imitated art. The two of them had been inseparable; as Zoe had once put it, they'd been Siamese twins joined at the lips.

'There's Luke, of course,' Fern said slowly. 'But that was such a long time ago. It hardly seems real now.'

Zoe nodded, jotting his name into her notebook. 'I know what you mean. I can hardly believe we were actually at college with him, never mind that we were best friends. An A-list Hollywood star, who'd have thought it?' She paused, her pen poised above the page. 'Do you know, I was reading in the papers only the other day that he's tipped to take the lead in that new action blockbuster. What's it called again?'

'*Dynamite*,' said Fern, who'd also read it and been thrilled for him. 'He's come a long way since the uni drama society, that's for sure.'

'He was always a fantastic actor, though,' Zoe recalled. 'I'm not really surprised he's made such a success of his career. And of course there's the fact that he's sex on a stick!'

'Mmm,' said Fern, prodding the panini with a fork. The cheese had congealed now and a pool of grease was spreading across the napkin. It didn't matter; she wasn't feeling hungry anyway. Thinking about her exes had that effect on Fern. Maybe she should market it as some kind of diet.

'Do you regret breaking up with Luke?' Zoe said gently.

Fern sighed. She had adored Luke. But, after university, they'd been pulled in different directions.

'Not really.' She twisted the large amber ring on her index finger. 'We wanted such different things and the timing was all wrong. Luke was desperate to pursue acting as a career and I wanted to concentrate on set design. I knew I couldn't do that if I was following him from place to place. And,' she sighed, 'I suppose part of me was sick of always being skint. I wanted to move on from renting tatty houses and always eating leftovers. Besides, Luke was too focused on Luke to understand that I could be equally focused on my career.'

'Luke's hardly a struggling impoverished thespian any longer,' pointed out Zoe. 'He's practically royalty these days.'

That was true. Barely a week passed now without Luke appearing in the tabloids or chatting to Jonathan Ross or Richard and Judy. He was constantly papped and written about in celebrity magazines, and only last weekend he'd been linked to gorgeous singer-turned-actress Trinity. He was way out of Fern's league these days.

Zoe drained her coffee. 'Okay, so there's Luke. Who else could Mr Right be? What about Matt? He was a sweet guy.'

Now it was Fern's turn to roll her eyes. 'Please, Zoe, spare me the St Matt of Putney lecture.'

'He was a nice guy! Honestly, Fern, sometimes I think you're impossible to please.'

Fern had dated Matt in her mid-twenties but the relationship had ended bitterly when Fern decided to take time out and go travelling. On paper Matt had been perfect boyfriend material: conventionally dark and handsome, polite, solvent and with a great career as a vet, but Fern had felt suffocated by the regularity of her life with him. When he'd begun to mention marriage and children and relocating to the countryside she'd started to panic. Travelling in the Far East had suddenly seemed like a very good idea. Matt, however, had been devastated . . .

She sighed. 'Matt was lovely, but he didn't want to travel with me, remember?'

Zoe wagged a French-manicured finger at Fern. 'You dumped Luke for not offering you any stability and then you moaned that Matt wasn't exciting enough. Luke travelled too much, Matt didn't travel enough. Bloody hell, Fern, what *do* you want?'

'I want it all, whatever it all actually is! The perfect balance, I suppose. And lovely as Matt was I was never going to find it with him, was I?'

'You had him and you let him go,' Zoe reminded her. 'There's a pattern emerging, babes. You're a serial dumper of men. You just dumped Cheating Bastard.'

Cheating Bastard a.k.a. Seb was top of Zoe's list of most hated things, beating even spiders and unreliable wedding caterers.

It was a dubious achievement.

'I didn't have much choice,' Fern said sadly. Every time she thought about Seb's betrayal it felt like she was pulling her insides out with pliers. Surely she shouldn't still be this upset about it? 'Do you think it's Seb?' Fern's emotional see-sawing was starting to make her feel queasy. 'He had a stable job but we did lots of exciting things together – that safari holiday he took me on was amazing – and he made me laugh loads.'

'He also made you cry loads.'

'True.' Fern traced patterns in the foam on her latte. 'He did have a great body, though.'

'Shame it's inhabited by a complete dick,' said Zoe tartly. 'No, you did totally the right thing dumping Seb. I'm sure the psychic wasn't referring to him.'

'What makes you think she's actually referring to anyone?' Fern's head was starting to pound. 'We're intelligent, educated, twenty-first-century women. This could all be total rubbish.'

'It could, but you said yourself that she knew too much for it to be a coincidence. You've found the love of your life and let him go, Fern. Are you prepared to risk ignoring that?'

Out on the river two swans glided past followed by four fluffy grey cygnets; on the opposite bank a young couple walked slowly along, pausing to steal kisses every few paces. As Zoe scribbled in her notebook the sunlight caught her diamond solitaire and sent rainbows darting over the table.

Fern closed her eyes. Was she willing to risk it?

'After all,' Zoe continued, 'the implication of "let him go" is that you can get him back again, isn't it?'

'Is it?'

'Of course! All we have to do is get you to speak to these guys again and then you're sure to be able to work out which one he is.'

'What's all this *we* stuff? And anyway, what about *your* prophecy?'

'Mine wasn't half as interesting as yours, babes. Besides, I'm practically an old married woman now so the only way I can get romance and excitement is through my single friends! Now, by happy coincidence two of your exes are already invited to the wedding. Sadly one is Cheating Bastard because he's a rugby mate of Steve's. Grrr.' Zoe grimaced. Fern knew for a fact that Zoe had fought Steve on that, but Steve, being the good guy he was, couldn't see his way to revoking a wedding invitation. 'The other one is Luke, who probably won't make it.'

Fern pulled a face. 'Just Seb then. Great.'

'I'm sure I could wangle an invite for Matt. He's the son of family friends, after all. We didn't include him in the first round but seeing as we've got a few people who can't make it I'm sure we could squeeze him in now. What do you think?'

Fern wasn't certain she actually wanted to see Matt again. Some of the things he'd said when they'd split up had been less than friendly. He was more likely to punch her on the nose than to reveal himself as the long-lost love of her life. On the other hand, had she been too hasty in dismissing him? Had she thrown away her chance of happiness just because he was too keen to settle down?

She couldn't bear that thought.

'After all,' Zoe ploughed on with all the delicacy of a steamroller in a china factory, 'you were always telling me how kind Matt was. Didn't he nurse you back to health when you broke your wrist? And wasn't it Matt who sent you flowers every day for the first month of your relationship?'

Fern nodded. At the time she'd felt like one of the kittens in his surgery and the flowers thing had driven her demented after a few days – it was no fun being stalked by Interflora – but looking back with rose-tinted spectacles firmly in place it was starting to look rather sweet. What if Matt was the one who'd got away?

Zoe was right. She couldn't risk it.

'Okay!' Fern said, a small knot of excitement starting to twist in her stomach. 'Invite him. It can't hurt to see him again, just in case.'

'That's the spirit.' Zoe grinned. 'I just know things are going to work out. I feel it in my bones. Let's have some more lattes to celebrate!'

As Zoe wove her way through the tables Fern placed her pounding head in her hands and tried to pop the rising bubbles of excitement. I need to get things into perspective, she told herself sternly. Just because a psychic told me I've already met the one doesn't mean it's true. But it was no good trying to be sensible. She didn't really do sensible – her platform boots were a bit of a giveaway there – but her intentions were good. As she closed her eyes and enjoyed the warmth of the sunlight on her face Angela's quiet, authoritative voice kept echoing in her mind.

'Zoe, you look stunning!' Fern gasped the following weekend, when she walked into the bedroom where the bride was putting the finishing touches to her outfit. Dressed in a simple white Vera Wang column dress with her blond hair swept into an elegant chignon Zoe was heartbreakingly beautiful and Fern's eyes filled.

'Is it okay?' Zoe's eyes met Fern's in the looking glass. 'You don't think I'm a bit over the hill to pull this off?' She fiddled with the white gardenia tucked behind her ear and then picked up the matching bouquet.

'You look beautiful,' Fern said, hugging her. 'Steve's one very lucky man. And as for being over the hill, I don't think I've ever heard such rubbish!'

'It was you who said you were too old to be a bridesmaid,' Zoe reminded her.

'Well, I am! Come on, I'd look hideous dressed in pink ruffles, like a lost loo roll holder!'

'Give me some credit. My bridesmaids are wearing cerise!'

Fern grinned. 'Silly me. That's nothing like pink! Anyway, your nieces will do a much better job than I ever could. I'd be bound to trip up as I went down the aisle and land in the font or something.'

Zoe glanced down at Fern's shoes – big green wedges today laced around her ankles with scarlet ribbons – and her mouth curled into a smile. Fern's penchant for dramatics and broken bones was well known amongst her friends.

'Besides,' she added, 'you know what they say about always being the bridesmaid. I'm not going to jeopardise my love life any further, thank you very much! Not when two of my potential lost soulmates are at this wedding.'

'About that,' began Zoe. 'I think you should know—'

But whatever she was about to say was cut short when her father came into the room, dressed in his morning suit and beaming from ear to ear at his radiant daughter.

'It's time to go,' he said, offering Zoe his arm to tuck her hand through. 'I can't believe my little girl is actually getting married!'

Fern's eyes welled up again. She was happy for Zoe, but part of her ached to think that her own father would never be there to walk her down the aisle.

Get a grip, she told herself sternly. Unless you find out who it was you let go the nearest you'll get to an aisle is shopping in Sainsbury's. She blew her friend a kiss. 'Good luck, Zoe. Enjoy every minute.' Then she slipped away from the room, trying very hard not to think about being in the same place as Matt and Seb. She'd be more at ease walking barefoot over hot coals.

I'm not going to think about them right now, she told herself firmly. This was Zoe's special day and she wanted to focus on every single second of it. Angela's prophecy had taken up way too much head space already.

Zoe and Steve had opted to hold their wedding in a beautiful country house hotel. The ceremony was taking place in the huge ballroom with the reception planned for the sumptuous dining room and, if the weather permitted, the guests could spill out on to the terrace and the garden. As Fern hurried down the sweeping staircase she admired the way the banisters had been woven with ivy, white roses and trailing cerise ribbons and heaved a sigh of relief that sunlight was spilling through the cupola above.

The bridesmaids waiting at the bottom of the stairs looked adorable in their cerise dresses and had gardenias and baby's breath woven into their hair. Fern couldn't help feeling glad that she'd declined to join them, though. She felt much more confident in the vintage red and green Liberty print dress she'd found in one of her favourite boutiques teamed with the green wedges to give her some height. And she could never master elegant chignons. Her curls could give Steve McQueen a run for his money when it came to escaping, so today she'd just pinned them loosely with a few tendrils framing her face and a red rose tucked behind her ear. Add to that a bra that was a miracle of engineering and granny pants Bridget Jones would be proud of and Fern was ready to do battle.

Or meet her exes.

Sitting down at the back of the room Fern shoved her red fluffy bag beneath the seat and glanced around. There was a low murmur of excited chatter above the gentle strains of the string quartet and by the door Zoe's wedding planner was issuing final instructions to the celebrant. Steve was sitting at the front of the room beneath a floral arch with his best man at his side, the rigid set of his shoulders speaking volumes about how nervous he was feeling.

Fern craned her neck a little and waved to Priya – much less green looking than the last time she'd seen her – and smiled at several familiar faces from university. The glossy red bob beneath the sage-green hat could only be Charlotte and there was Libby next to Mrs Forster, looking quite unlike her usual skater girl self in a stunning Grecian-style creation. Fern felt a little less guilty knowing that she wasn't the only adult who'd been disinclined to don a bridesmaid's dress and abandon her dignity for several hours, although she suspected that if Libby had been allowed to wear cerise combats and Sketchers there wouldn't have been an issue.

Scanning the room like a frock-wearing version of *The Terminator* Fern finally spotted a familiar dark curly head. Instantly, her heart took a trip to her mouth. Matt was sitting two rows in front of her, a little stockier maybe than he'd been four years ago and perhaps his hair was longer than she remembered but it was undeniably him. Fern closed her eyes and remembered how it had felt to wind her fingers into the soft curls at the nape of his neck and the way that his lips had traced gentle kisses along her collarbone, grazing upwards across the soft skin of her throat and then to the corner of her mouth.

She was starting to remember exactly what it was she'd seen in Matt before his dependability and seriousness had started to make her feel trapped. She felt like kicking herself with one of her wedges, except the injury could be lethal.

It was so annoying. Why didn't anyone tell you that what you wanted in your twenties wasn't necessarily what you wanted in your thirties?

A beautiful willowy brunette was sitting next to Matt. From the closeness of their bodies Fern guessed that she was probably his girlfriend. Was it serious between them, she wondered, or was she just a date for the wedding?

'Excuse me, is this seat taken?'

Fern almost jumped out of her skin because there was Seb, leaning over her bare shoulder and smiling down at her. His smoky dark grey eyes were glittering with emotion and his one-hundred-watt smile was as charming as ever. Fern resisted the Pavlovian impulse to smile back. How could she ever have thought seeing Seb again was a good idea? It was the emotional equivalent of ripping out stitches.

'You look fantastic,' Seb said, taking Fern's

silence for acquiescence and sitting down next to her. 'That's a stunning dress. Have you lost weight?'

'Yes,' snapped Fern. 'I've lost twelve stone of useless male.'

'You're still angry.' Seb sighed. 'Baby, how many times can I say it? I'm so sorry. It meant nothing to me, you know that.'

Actually, Fern did know that. Seb really was to guilt what Teflon was to grease. But the point was his affair with Vanessa *had* meant something to Fern. When she'd attended one of his work dos and overheard two women discussing his fling with Vanessa, and how bad they felt for Fern, she'd felt a pain so hard and sharp that she'd thought she might pass out. If it wasn't too much of a cliché Fern would have said it was her heart breaking.

Not that she'd ever give Seb the satisfaction of knowing just how much he'd hurt her. Clinging to what shreds of dignity she had left – after all he'd seen her screaming and had to dodge the Le Creuset wok she'd hurled at his head – Fern dug her nails into her palms and fought to keep her temper.

'I'm not discussing this right now,' she hissed. 'It's a wedding, Seb. They're supposed to be happy occasions, remember?'

'Sorry. You're right.' Instantly Seb's handsome

features were composed into a contrite expression and his eyes looked so sad that a basset hound looked cheerful by comparison. 'It's just that I miss you so much, Fern. I really do. I can't stop thinking about you.'

Fern ignored him. Luckily at this point the string quartet broke into *Ave Maria*, heralding the arrival of the bride. As Zoe and her father walked slowly along the aisle towards Steve, Fern did her best to push all thoughts of prophecies and exes aside. Tears filled her eyes as she saw the look of love that passed between the bride and groom.

There and then Fern Moss made herself a very solemn promise: nothing but a love like that was going to do.

She was never going to settle for second best.

Steve raised his glass of champagne and cleared his throat.

'To my wonderful new wife. Mrs Zoe Kent!'

'Mrs Zoe Kent!' echoed the wedding guests, raising their glasses to the top table and sighing as Steve kissed his smiling bride.

Fern took a big gulp of champagne and blinked. Honestly, what was the matter with her today? Her eyes were filling up so often you could stick her in a toy shop and call her Tiny Tears. She'd had welling eyes all the way through the ceremony too. She'd never heard anything as romantic as Zoe and Steve exchanging their vows. Zoe had looked utterly radiant, her eyes sparkling and her cheeks flushed as Steve tenderly placed the ring on her finger and promised to love and cherish her for ever.

Lucky Zoe to have found someone who felt that

way about her, Fern had thought wistfully. At least when it had got to the 'forsaking all others' part Seb had had the good grace to look down at his shoes while Fern fought the urge to beat him to death with her order of service.

Still, somehow she'd made it through the ceremony without strangling him and now the reception was in full swing. The speeches were over, the guests pleasantly full of boeuf en croûte and marbled chocolate mousse, and gradually people were spilling out through the French windows. Beyond the terrace the trees had been festooned with pink and white fairy lights which twinkled like a thousand stars while the gentle strains of the string quartet drifted upwards towards heaven. It was simply perfect.

Excusing herself to the other guests at her table, Fern made her way on to the terrace and leaned her elbows against the lichen-crusted stone. The gardens dropped away below, all smoky blues and purples in the gathering dusk, while above a small slice of moon played hide and seek with the clouds.

'Beautiful,' Seb said from the shadows behind her.

Fern started and then nodded. 'It's been a beautiful wedding.'

'I'm not talking about the wedding,' he said softly. 'I meant what I said earlier, Fern. You look absolutely gorgeous. I'm so sorry things went wrong between us.'

'Things didn't *go wrong* between us!' Fern spun round angrily. 'You screwed another woman, Seb! It wasn't exactly an accident!'

Seb hung his head. 'You're right, babe. I was a total idiot and I made a mistake.'

Fern felt a familiar stabbing pain beneath her breastbone. During the first few weeks after breaking up with Seb that pain had been her constant companion. She'd thought it had gone, but after only minutes back in his company it was slicing into her anew.

Maybe she wasn't quite as over him as she'd hoped.

'Forgetting someone's birthday or dialling the wrong number is a mistake,' she said stiffly. 'Not sleeping with somebody else. How on earth can that be a mistake when it was something you actively chose to do?'

'How many times can I say it? I'm really sorry.'

'Sorry?' Fern echoed incredulously. 'Seb, you slept with someone else and all you can say is that you're *sorry*? Don't you get it? Saying you're *sorry* doesn't make everything better. Saying *sorry* doesn't change anything!'

'I know that.' Seb tried to put a hand on her shoulder but Fern flinched away. Once there'd been a time when she'd loved his touch. He'd been able to turn her insides to melting ice cream just by the slightest brushing of his fingers against her skin, but since Vanessa close proximity to Seb made her skin crawl. How did he ever think he could mend things between them? She'd rather be locked in a broom cupboard with Osama bin Laden than spend another second with Seb.

'Just leave me alone,' she told him wearily. 'I've heard it all before and it was bad enough the first time round.'

Seb grabbed her by the shoulders and stared down at her. His eyes were as pewter grey as a storm-tossed sea. 'It was a mistake, Fern, a stupid, drunken mistake. I swear to God, if you give me a second chance I'll never screw up again. I love you!'

'You love me so you shagged someone else? How the hell do you figure that out?'

'It didn't mean anything, sweetheart.'

'Well it bloody well meant something to me!' snapped Fern, shaking him off. 'And it probably meant something to Vanessa too.'

Seb passed a hand over his face. 'Okay. I understand. You're angry with me. I deserve it.'

'Damn right I'm angry!' Fern glared at him. It didn't matter any longer that he was handsome and witty and possibly the best lover she'd ever had. She'd set herself a new ground rule: no more men who were good in bed and useless everywhere else. And Seb for all his good points was pretty bloody useless. Even after they'd split up he still didn't understand why his betrayal had left her so hurt and angry.

'Can't we put this behind us and try again?' Seb pleaded, taking one of Fern's small ring-covered hands in his. 'We were good together, weren't we?'

In spite of herself Fern nodded. Life with Seb had seemed the perfect balance of excitement and stability. She'd adored him.

Note the past tense, she told herself sternly.

'So how about you forgive me and we try again? I know we could make it work. You love me and I love you. What could be simpler?'

Fern snatched her hand away. With Seb she'd always felt she was hitting her head against a brick wall and some things never changed.

'You really don't get it, do you? You betrayed me in the worst way possible. I don't think I can forgive you however much I might want to. And even if I could forgive I don't think I'd ever be able to forget.'

Seb stared at her, taken aback. 'I don't know what more I can say, except I'm sorry.'

'Will you please stop saying you're sorry!' To her dismay Fern discovered that her throat was contracting with tears. The number she'd shed over Seb already, there ought to be a world shortage.

'Oh, Fern, please don't cry,' Seb begged. 'I can't bear it. I never meant to hurt you, darling.'

'It's a bit late for that,' Fern choked. 'Look, Seb, there's really no point in going over and over old ground. The bottom line is that you cheated on me and I don't think I'll ever be able to get over it. I just can't be with you any more. In fact I can hardly bear to look at you.'

She spun round on her heel, a sob tightening her throat, and strode across the terrace, or maybe scuttled was a more accurate description of moving at speed in the killer wedges.

Bloody, bloody Seb. How typical that he'd expect her to welcome him back with open arms even after he'd slept with another woman. The guy was as sensitive as a charging rhino in full body armour. Maybe in the past they'd always made up after rowing but not this time, she thought angrily, dashing tears away with the back of her hand and hurtling down some steps on to the parterre. Seb couldn't possibly be the one she'd let go. It must be one of the other two, it had to be! She could never go back to Seb.

There was no way he was her soulmate.

Below on the parterre it was quiet and shadowy. The further Fern walked from the terrace the faster her tears fell. She tried hard to hold them back, fearing that once she started she'd never stop, but Seb's words kept buzzing through her memory like apologetic wasps. Sinking on to a stone bench she buried her face in her hands. What a waste of what once had been a good relationship. How could Seb have thrown it away so carelessly?

The tinkle of glasses and the muffled murmur of conversations drifted on the breeze. Fern took a shaky breath. This was supposed to be a happy occasion. There was no way she was going to let Seb wreck her enjoyment of Zoe's special day. She'd sit here for a few minutes and get herself together, then she'd go back to the reception, wash her face and throw herself into the celebrations. She wasn't going to spend her best friend's wedding hiding in the garden weeping over her ex. It was time she actually caught up with Zoe. Several times during the reception Zoe had waved and beckoned her over, but each time Fern tried to approach the bride was swept away by photographers or proud relatives. She'd yet to even congratulate the new Mrs Kent.

As Fern's breathing started to slow and become less ragged she was aware that she was no longer alone. Her hands curled into fists. She wasn't certain what the word was for killing your ex-boyfriend but she was pretty sure she'd soon find out if this was Seb coming back for a second round of apologies.

'Fern?' said a voice from the shadows, low and rich as sticky toffee pudding. 'Is that you?'

She started. In the evening stillness she could almost hear the crackling of emotional static.

The man standing on the lawn was an ex all right, but he wasn't Seb. Matt was staring at her, an expression of mingled horror and embarrassment flitting across his face. For a split second he looked as though he might back away. Fern wouldn't have blamed him if he had; they'd hardly parted on friendly terms, after all. Suddenly very conscious of her wet cheeks and smeared mascara she attempted to wipe her eyes with her fingers. Why had she chosen to wear a sleeveless dress? She had nothing to dry her eyes with. Matt might have been her boyfriend once but Fern drew the line at blowing her nose on her skirt in front of him.

'Hey, you're crying.' Noticing Fern's tear-stained face Matt's first instinct was to help. Stepping forward, he sat awkwardly next to her and offered her his jacket cuff. 'I haven't got a hanky, I'm afraid,' he said ruefully.

Half laughing and half sobbing Fern accepted his sleeve gratefully and mopped up her tears. Dear old Matt. She'd treated him so badly when she longed for excitement and adventure but here he was, by her side in her time of need. Those dependable qualities that had once seemed so cloying and so suffocating now seemed reassuring and solid.

'Better?' he asked.

She gave him a watery smile. 'Much better, thanks. You can have your sleeve back now.'

'Sure?' Matt smiled back and Fern found herself remembering what a wide and generous mouth he had. 'I've got another one if you like.'

'I'm fine. God, I'm sorry, Matt. You didn't need to walk into me having an emotional meltdown.'

He shrugged. 'I seem to recall that the last time we met *I* was the one in emotional meltdown.'

Ouch. Fern wasn't sure what to say to that. *I know* sounded arrogant and *I'm sorry* was totally inadequate.

'Matt, I—'

'Sorry, Fern, I shouldn't have said that. It's all water under the bridge. I'm not going to start berating you now, I promise.'

'So you're not about to boil my bunny?' Fern tried to joke.

'Certainly not. I'm a vet!' Matt said, pulling a serious face. 'Honestly, it's fine. I don't hold any grudges about what happened between us. You were right anyway, as it turned out; we would never have worked as a couple. We're far too different. Amanda and I are much better suited.'

Amanda? That must be the slender brunette he was sitting with during the wedding service. 'That's great.'

They sat in charged silence for several minutes. Fern's heart was heavy. What if this kind, gentle man was the one she'd let go? Wouldn't that just be bloody typical?

'And are you seeing anyone?' he asked eventually.

She shrugged her slim shoulders. 'There was someone but it didn't really work out the way I'd hoped.'

'The guy on the terrace?' Matt asked. 'Is he the reason you're upset?'

'It's a long story. Let's just say he found a better option.'

Matt's dark eyebrows shot into his curly brown hair. 'I find that hard to believe. A guy would have to look a long way to find someone better than you, Fern.'

'Really?' she whispered.

'Really.' He nodded. 'I loved you, Fern. You're funny, and unique, and so sexy. My little blonde imp was how I always used to think of you, because you always made me laugh with all the mischief you used to get up to. Finding anyone who could measure up to you would be a tall bloody order.'

'But you have,' she sighed.

'I couldn't wait for you for ever, could I?'

Yes! Fern wanted to shout. That's exactly what you should have done if you're the love of my life! But of course Matt had moved on. He was kind and funny and good looking; perfect partner material. What had she been thinking to throw this guy away on a whim?

And what exactly was he trying to say? Did he mean that he'd wanted to wait for her? Did he still regret their break-up? Fern took a deep breath. Life was too short to hang around.

'Matt! There you are, honey!' Just as she was plucking up the courage to ask Matt exactly what he meant the willowy brunette wandered across the smooth lawn towards them and the intimate moment vanished like mist in sunlight.

'Sorry, darling!' Jumping up from the bench Matt took the brunette's hand in his and dropped a tender kiss on the top of her head. 'I was just catching up with an old friend.'

'So I see,' said Amanda, her narrowed brown eyes suggesting she'd already guessed exactly what kind of old friend Fern was. 'Aren't you going to introduce us?'

'Of course,' said Matt quickly. 'Fern, I'd like you to meet Amanda, my future wife.'

Fern was glad that she was sitting down. 'Sorry? What did you say?'

'This is my fiancée, Amanda,' Matt repeated, raising Amanda's left hand to display a large diamond solitaire. 'She's been brave enough to agree to take me on.'

'Wow! Congratulations!' Genuinely lost for words, all Fern could do was smile at the happy couple while mentally slapping herself on the forehead. To think she'd thought Matt had been on the brink of admitting he still had feelings for her. That champagne must be stronger than she'd realised. She'd make sure she got another glass as soon as possible and hopefully drink herself into oblivion somewhere where her exes couldn't find her, she decided, before she made a total prat of herself.

'Matt and I got engaged last week,' Amanda said proudly, gazing down at her ring. 'It was so romantic! Can you believe that he flew me all the way to Paris and proposed by the Eiffel Tower?'

Fern could totally believe it. It sounded exactly like the kind of cliché that Matt had loved. It was this predictable side of him that had often made her teeth itch with irritation. 'That sounds amazing!' she said dutifully.

'Indeed it was.' Losing interest in Fern now that she'd staked her claim, Amanda wound her arm through Matt's and smiled up at him. 'I was just saying to Zoe earlier that she must give us the details of this hotel. Wouldn't it be perfect for our engagement dinner, darling?'

Ah. Now Fern understood why Zoe had been beckoning so frantically. She must have been terrified that Fern was about to make a total idiot of herself.

It wouldn't have been the first time.

'Er, yes, perfect,' said Matt, but although the words were addressed to Amanda his eyes held Fern's, and in spite of the warm night air she shivered. There was unfinished business with Matt, that was for sure. The atmosphere between them was granite heavy.

'Anyway, darling, I came to fetch you in because they're about to cut the cake,' said Amanda. 'I really wanted us to see how Zoe and Steve have planned it. We need to think about our wedding now! I can hardly believe how much there is to do.' She laced her fingers through his. 'It was nice to meet you, Fran.'

'Yeah, nice to meet you too,' muttered Fern as Amanda towed Matt back across the parterre. Something told her that was one wedding she wouldn't be getting an invite to.

Now, what looked better? The red satin scarf or the green velvet throw? Fern stepped back from the chaise longue, her brow crinkled in thought and her teeth worrying her top lip. The heroine of this latest period drama, *Josephine*, was to be draped languidly across the sofa for what the script promised would be a very steamy scene indeed and Fern's job as set designer was to get every detail exactly right. She had to create the perfect background for some of the most erotic scenes you could find on the BBC and she was starting to wonder if she was really the right girl for the job, because reading that scene was the closest she had come to passion for quite a while. The state her love life was in she couldn't help thinking she'd be better off dressing the set of *Casualty*.

Narrowing her eyes, Fern took another step back.

Every detail was perfect, from the Louise Quinze replica furniture to the marble-effect fireplace. Even the thick Turkish rugs were exactly what the director had visualised, so why couldn't she decide on the bloody throw? She blamed the trauma of meeting two of her most significant exes at Zoe's wedding. Two weeks on Fern was still in a spin about Angela's words and the nagging suspicion that Matt could well be the one she'd let go. Normally her natural inclination would have been to do something dramatic to decide the issue one way or another, but the fact Matt had a fiancée put the lid on that particular idea.

'Arrgh!' she screeched, hurling herself and the green velvet throw on to the chaise longue in a fit of frustration. 'What am I going to do?'

'Abandon that revolting green and come for lunch, that's what!' replied a laughing voice. 'You know you want to!'

'Alek!' Delighted, Fern leapt up from the sofa and hurled herself into the arms of the slender dark-haired man who was grinning at her across the set. 'When did you get back? Are you here for long? How's Prague?'

Alek laughed. After two years of working with Fern he was used to her tendency to gabble away nineteen to the dozen.

'An hour ago. No. And it's great!'

'It's so good to see you!' said Fern, feeling all her annoyance with throws and prophecies vanish in an instant now that one of her best friends was back. Aleksander Novak had been her sounding board, her partner in crime and possibly one of the most talented set designers she'd ever been lucky enough to work with. She'd not met anyone anywhere near as good since he'd left the year before. Although she'd been really sad, she'd understood that he'd wanted to be nearer to his Czech girlfriend. Besides, at that time if Seb had suggested moving to Mars she'd have gone like a shot, so she totally understood why Prague had been impossible to resist.

'It's good to see you too,' said Alek, hugging her tightly. 'So good. I've really missed you. Hey!' He frowned down at her. 'You've lost weight.'

'Don't you start,' said Fern sternly. 'It's called the ex plan and I really don't recommend it. If you take me to the noodle bar I promise I'll eat as much as you can cram down my throat.'

'The noodle bar!' Alek's dark eyes grew dreamy. 'God, I've missed that place. I'm already tasting strips of chicken in black bean sauce! Let's go.'

'I can't go anywhere until I've finished this set.' Fern sighed, slipping out of his embrace and frowning again at the throws. She shook her head with frustration. 'I just can't get this right and I can't figure out why. Nothing's working.'

Alek folded his arms and looked thoughtfully at the set. The hot studio lights bounced off his cheekbones and glistened from his jet-black hair. His chiselled face was all planes and angles. Fern had often thought that he looked just like a Cherokee Indian, albeit a Slavic one.

Alek was striding around the set, appraising her handiwork through narrowed sloe-hued eyes.

'Hmm, I'm thinking opulence? Seduction? Yet also romance? But trying not to look too obvious?'

'You've got it.' Fern wasn't surprised, because Alek had always been able to read her mind. It was what had made them such a great team. 'I'm trying to avoid cliché like mad, which is why I'm baulking at the satins and velvets.'

'Right, I understand.' He looked from the set to Fern and then back again. 'Can I suggest something?'

'Please do,' Fern said.

Stepping forward Alek picked up a corner of the vintage cream and gold brocade scarf that Fern was wearing over her plain black vest and flowing scarlet gypsy skirt. In one fluid motion he plucked it from her shoulders and draped it on the chaise longue, transforming the set from obviously sexy to demure yet alluring with one flick of his wrist.

Fern exhaled in awe. 'I've missed you, Mr Novak. You're a genius.'

Alek grinned at her. 'It has been said, Ms Moss! But for you I will not charge my usual extortionate fee. You can pay me in noodles for my skills. Let's go for lunch!'

And the hungry Fern didn't need asking twice.

'Was I right or was I right about these noodles?' Alek looked smug as he watched Fern fork up her food like there was about to be a world noodle shortage. 'Aren't they divine?'

Fern nodded, unable to speak because her mouth was too full of the scrummiest noodles ever tasted. Tossed in sesame oil and coated with just a splash of soy sauce, they were exactly what she'd needed after her hectic morning. Throw in the tenderest strips of chicken and the crunchiest mangetouts and there you had it: noodle heaven.

'So, am I forgiven for moving away?' Alek asked.

Fern swallowed noodles and dabbed at her mouth with a napkin. 'There's nothing to forgive, Alek. It was the perfect opportunity for you. You'd have been mad not to take it.'

'Have you missed me, though?' He raised an eyebrow. 'Come on, Fern; tell me that you can't live without me and that your life in set design is now a barren wilderness.'

'Yeah, right!' Fern scoffed. 'I've hardly noticed you've gone!'

'How cruel she is,' Alek remarked to himself, twisting noodles idly round his fork. 'I think about her every day, tell myself that I cannot live without my good friend Fern for a second longer, and what does she do? She tells me that she does not miss me. She breaks my heart!'

Fern rolled her eyes. 'And when you're not dying of loneliness how's it actually going out in Prague? Still enjoying it?'

He lit up like a Christmas tree. 'It's amazing. The Prague office is expanding on a daily basis. Seriously, Fern, you would not believe how lucrative set design is out there.'

'I'm so pleased it's all worked out for you.' She tapped at the Rolex on his wrist. 'And you don't need to tell me how well it pays. I can see that for myself.'

Alek flushed. 'Is it too posey? I promised myself one if we broke even after the first year. I never expected us to be making a profit after only six months.'

'I'm teasing!' Fern laughed. 'You've worked hard so enjoy every minute of your success. I'm thrilled for you, Al. It sounds amazing.'

'It could be a lot better, though,' he said thoughtfully, looking up at her. 'I have a great team in Prague but there's something missing. Or do I mean somebody?'

Fern wagged a finger. 'Alek, don't start all that please-move-to-Prague stuff again.'

'Oh, Fern, why ever not? I really need you there! There's nobody with your unique creative flair, or the passion to spend all day sourcing exactly the right shade of paint. And try as I might I can't find anyone who is able to drive in platform boots or looks as good as you do in a fluffy miniskirt. Come on, Fern. Please come and work for me. We'd have a brilliant time!'

Alek had never been much good at subtlety. For the last six months his texts and emails and phone calls had been filled with concrete-heavy hints about moving to Prague to become a partner in the business. Fern was seriously torn. She loved the idea of working with him again; they'd always been a brilliant team and no one made her laugh like Alek. He was one of the few people she knew who didn't despair of her crazy dramatics but actually joined in.

The adventures they'd had getting on the wrong trains or mistakenly turning up to serious parties in fancy dress would fill a book, and when Alek left Fern had shed many tears over losing such a kindred spirit. It would be a lot of fun to hang out with him again, and she was also very tempted by the thought of living abroad. Much as she loved Tooting it hardly compared with Prague when it came to history and romance, did it?

'Come and work with me,' said Alek, sensing her indecision and going for the jugular. 'You'd love it in Prague, Fern, and Chess and I would show you round and introduce you to everyone. We have a fantastic social life and you'd have a lot of fun. Come on, my chick. You only live once!' He paused as an idea took shape. 'Hey, you could move in with me and Chess. We'd have so much fun!'

Francesca, with her porcelain complexion and waist-length chestnut hair, always made Fern think of Lara from *Dr Zhivago* and on the few occasions they'd met she and Fern had got on really well, partly because Alek and Fern had never muddied the waters of their friendship by dating and also because they had mutual friends. But lovely and welcoming as Chess was Fern didn't relish the thought of being an awkward third person butting into her life with Alek. She'd had enough gooseberry moments with Steve and Zoe to last a lifetime.

No, Fern decided sadly as she stared down at her congealing noodles, she was thirty-one, not twenty-one, and much as the idea of moving to Prague appealed maybe it was time she started thinking about her own plans. Unfashionable as it sounded she wanted to settle down and have a family of her own in the not-so-distant future, and that was hardly going to happen if she was away gallivanting all over the Czech Republic with Alek. Besides, how could she turn her back on her mission to rediscover her one true love? How could she possibly move abroad before she'd worked out which one of the three it really was?

'Come on, Fern,' said Alek, reaching across the table and taking her small hand in his. 'I'm serious. I'd love nothing more than for you to come and work with me in Prague. Just name your salary and I'll double it – triple it, even. Go on, what's to stop you? You're not with Seb any more and you're not seeing anyone else, are you?'

'No, I'm still a spinster of the parish,' she sighed. 'And with my track record that's not about to change any time soon.'

'Then all the men in England are stupid and

need their eyes tested,' said Alek gallantly. 'Sod all of them and come out to Prague! We've got loads of single friends who'd love to go out with you.'

Right, thought Fern, that settled it. There was no way she was moving abroad to play the lonely singleton to Alek's Cilla Black! Anyway, she wasn't going to give up on finding out who her one true love was before she'd even started. Her mother was always accusing her of going off half cocked and she was determined to live down that reputation. It wasn't her fault that she always seemed to attract disasters.

'It's not that simple, Alek,' she said.

'Why isn't it? If you want to do something then just do it,' said Alek, for whom life really was that black and white. Offered a job in Prague? Then take it. Fancy a stunning girl? Just ask her out. Problem with a set? Easy, drape a scarf over a chair and it's fixed. It must be nice to live in Alek Land, thought Fern. What a pain that she lived in Fern World where life had a nasty habit of biting you on the bum. Like letting you lose the love of your life, for example . . .

For a second Fern toyed with the idea of telling Alek about Angela's prophecy. They were good friends, after all, so how was it different from confiding in Zoe? But just as she was on the verge of opening her mouth she remembered how scathing

Alek always was when she read her horoscope and how he'd laughed like a drain when she and Zoe had scared themselves silly watching *Most Haunted*.

Hmm. Maybe not then.

'Come on, Fern,' Alek was saying, his hand holding hers tightly now. 'Make a change. You know you want to.'

She sighed and slid her fingers away. 'I can't. I've got obligations, Alek, and I couldn't just up sticks and move away even if I wanted to, which I'm not saying I do before you jump in and say I could!' Alek mimed zipping up his mouth as Fern carried on. 'I've got contracts with work, I've signed a year's lease on my flat and there's my family too. I'd hate to leave my nieces behind, I'd really miss them, and my other sister's having a baby next month too. And what about my mum? You know how unstable she is. It really isn't as easy as all that, not for me, anyway.'

'Okay! Okay!' He held up his hands in surrender. 'I understand what you're saying. I won't hassle you any more if you really have made your mind up.'

'I have,' Fern told him. She really had. It was time to stop running the way she'd run away from Matt. Maybe it was time she stuck around and tried harder to be more grown up and responsible. That seemed to have worked for her sisters Tamsin and

Chloe, whereas Fern's mother had spent most of her life gadding from one useless man or hare-brained scheme to another and it didn't seem to have made her very happy. Fern didn't want to wake up in thirty years and be a carbon copy of Cybil Moss.

Why couldn't there be a balance between the two ways of life? she thought sadly as Alek paid the bill and walked her back to work. Did women always have to make a choice between family and career? Why couldn't she have the best of both worlds?

Answers on a postcard please.

'You know my offer still stands if you want it to,' Alek told her softly as he kissed her goodbye and folded her into a farewell hug.

'Thanks, Alek,' she murmured. 'It's really kind of you.'

'It isn't kind, it's bloody selfish. I meant every word I said. You'd be an asset to the team and I'd love to have you nearer. You can change you mind any time, Fern.'

'I'll bear it in mind,' she promised, hugging him back but knowing in her heart that her mind was already made up. She was going to stay put, be a good daughter and sister, and she was going to find the love of her life.

Wasn't she?

'Oh no, not again!'

Fern stood on her doorstep, car keys in her hand and her green beaded bag on her shoulder, and stared aghast at the large bunch of indigo alliums. Not that there was anything wrong with the bouquet, or the three identical arrangements that had been delivered already. Alliums were her favourite flowers and usually she'd have been over the moon to receive such beautiful bouquets.

No, Fern didn't have a problem with the bouquets but she did have an issue with the person who'd hand-delivered them every weekend since Zoe's wedding.

Seb, it seemed, was not prepared to take no for an answer.

She looked up and down the street but there was no sign of his blue BMW. Fern sighed with relief. It was half past ten in the morning and she was just about to head up the M40 to Oxfordshire for a family Sunday lunch. The last thing she felt like doing was performing another relationship autopsy with the pleading Seb.

It was such a shame he hadn't liked her this much when they'd actually been together.

Fern picked up the bouquet, kicked her front door shut and hopped over the low brick wall between her garden and that of the house next door. Luckily her neighbour, Freda, also liked alliums. She'd had to really in recent weeks because Fern certainly didn't want to keep them.

'Special delivery,' said Fern when her neighbour answered the bell.

'Oh dear!' Freda shook her grey head. 'He's not giving up easily, is he?'

'Sadly not.' Fern held out the bouquet. 'Could you give these a good home for me, please? I really don't think I can bear looking at them.'

'Are you quite sure you don't want them?' Freda buried her nose in the blooms. 'They're absolutely exquisite.'

'God, no! I feel guilty enough just looking at them on the doorstep.'

Freda fixed Fern with a steely gaze. 'You haven't

anything to feel guilty about, my dear girl! Don't you dare let this emotional blackmail get to you. You think back to the state you were in when you first moved in here and then tell me how guilty you feel.'

Just the mention of that bleak time after splitting up with Seb was enough to make Fern shudder. Numb with grief and shock, she'd lost not only the man she'd loved but her home too, as she'd been living with Seb in his gorgeous riverside apartment. The sparsely furnished garden flat she'd rented instead had seemed a cold and lonely place in comparison and Fern had spent her first night alone watching the shadows pool across the floor and crying so hard she'd looked like a frog. If it hadn't been for her quirky and occasionally fierce next-door neighbour Fern thought she'd probably still be weeping into her very sodden pillow. But confirmed singleton Freda had no intention of letting that happen and before long she'd taken her sad new neighbour under her wing. Many cups of tea and all-men-are-bastards chats later the two were firm friends, the thirty-year age gap vanishing as Freda told Fern stories about her childhood in Sweden or they rummaged together through the vintage boutiques in Spitalfields.

And Freda was also great for looking after Seb's unwanted flowers even if she wasn't his number one fan.

'Fair point, Free. My guilt's gone.' Fern grinned.

'Good girl.' Freda nodded approvingly. 'My, you do look lovely today. I love that green velvet dress. It looks great with those huge boots of yours. Are you going somewhere special?'

'I'm going for Sunday lunch at my sister Tamsin's place. We've all been summoned, even my mother.' She glanced at her battered Snoopy watch. 'Damn! It's nearly eleven already. Tamsin will freak if I'm late again.'

'Drive carefully,' called Freda, as Fern tore down the garden path. 'And don't forget your AA membership needs renewing. I'm not driving all the way to Banbury to rescue you again!'

Blowing her neighbour a kiss Fern let herself into her Beetle. She really would sort out the AA cover just as soon as she'd paid off her Barclaycard. And Visa. And maybe cleared her overdraft again . . .

Firing up the ignition and slotting an Abba cassette into the tape player Fern sent up a prayer that the car would make it all the way to Oxfordshire. She didn't fancy having to flag down a hunky lorry driver and hitch all the way to Tamsin's, although it wouldn't be the first time.

*

An hour and a half later a very relieved Fern pulled up outside her sister's pretty cottage in the small village of Upton Norton. After much excitement on the part of her nieces and an introduction to the family's new retriever puppy she was able to collapse at the scrubbed pine table with an icy glass of wine while Tamsin, a natural mother, performed marvels at the Aga and Chloe put the finishing touches to an apple pie. Laughingly turning down Fern's offers to help – her lack of domestic ability was a long-standing family joke – Tamsin insisted that she just relax after the long drive.

'I love it here, it's so peaceful,' sighed Fern, looking round the homely kitchen with pleasure. Tamsin's cottage could have come straight from *Country Living* magazine. Burnished copper pans hung from the oak-beamed ceiling, saucepans bubbled merrily on the cherry-red Aga and a clock tick-tocked away the time on the old Welsh dresser.

'Not at feeding time!' Tamsin laughed. 'Hungry children and husbands make a lot of noise. You just wait, Chloe. It's your turn soon.'

Chloe, who was eight months pregnant with her first baby, smiled and patted her bump. 'It's too late to change my mind now, Tam! I'll just make Dominic do all the feeding.'

'Good old Dominic, I bet he will too,' Tamsin said. 'In fact I'm only surprised he hasn't offered to give birth for you.'

'Where is the golden boy?' asked Fern. It was generally agreed in the Moss family that Chloe had found the perfect man. Accountant Dominic had perfect manners, perfect fair good looks and, if Chloe were to be believed, perfect technique in bed too, although that was a piece of information too far in Fern's opinion.

'He's just popped out with James to pick up some more wine,' Chloe said. 'Wish I could have a glass.'

It was on the tip of Fern's tongue to say she'd gladly swap a measly glass of wine for a loving husband and a baby on the way, but she stopped herself in time. It wasn't exactly that she was jealous of Chloe: Dominic with his attention to detail and tendency to iron creases in his jeans would wind her up so that she'd be ticking before very long with him. It was more that Fern was jealous of what Chloe and Tamsin *had* than a case of envying them their partners. If only she hadn't been so careless as to let her own soulmate go who knew what her life could have been like? Perhaps she and Matt would be here now with a brood of dark-eyed, mop-headed children. She sighed and took a big glug of wine to numb the stinging sense of loss.

Moving a joint of beef to the warming oven and popping the apple pie in to cook, Tamsin helped herself to a glass of wine and joined her sisters at the table. Outside, the girls and the puppy were tearing around the garden, shrieks and barks punctuating the still afternoon.

'Right,' said Tamsin, 'that's lunch taken care of for a bit.' She smiled at Fern, a kind motherly smile. 'So have you had any more success figuring out this prophecy of yours?'

The three Moss sisters were close, which was probably a legacy of being dragged around Europe by their mother after their father's death and having to take care of each other while Cybil gadded about with her latest beau. They shared everything, and for the past few weeks had discussed Angela's words at length as they tried to work out who it was Fern had let go. Romantic Chloe had her money on first love Luke, whereas the more practical Tamsin was firmly in favour of Matt, although Fern suspected this had something to do with cut-price vet bills.

She fiddled with her silver bangles. 'I've got absolutely no idea who he is except that it can't be Seb.'

'Absolutely not!' agreed Tamsin. 'There's no way he's the one, not after what he did to you. Bastard.'

'Yes, bastard,' echoed Chloe.

'I keep wondering whether it's Matt after all? At Zoe's wedding he seemed to be saying he still had feelings for me but he's engaged so I really can't ask him anything else. It wouldn't be fair.' Fern started to gnaw at her thumbnail. 'I'm a bit stuck now, if I'm honest.'

Tamsin leaned over and firmly removed Fern's thumb from her mouth. 'Stop it. That's a beastly habit.'

'You'd be chewing your nails too if your future depended on figuring out who you'd thrown away!'

Tamsin's brow furrowed. 'You seem to have really bought into this whole prophecy thing, hon. Maybe you ought to leave it to fate? What will be will be, and all that?'

'Bollocks!' said Chloe. 'She's got to meet her destiny head on. Right, Fern?'

'I'm not sure,' Fern sighed. 'Knowing my luck I'll probably go tripping over the free-will carpet and bring this whole destiny thing crashing down round me. Maybe Tam's right and I should just see what happens.'

'That's crap!' shrieked Chloe. 'What on earth's got into you?'

'Calm down, Clo. Watch your blood pressure,' Tamsin warned.

'Bugger my blood pressure!' exploded Chloe, her eyes wide with passion and her curls flying as she shook her head in disbelief. 'You never used to be so passive, Fern. You're normally always the first person to grab life by the balls. What about that time when we were in Sorrento? Don't tell me you've forgotten?'

Fern closed her eyes. She remembered it so well that sometimes if she smelt just the faintest hint of frangipani she was fifteen again, tanned and bored in the hot Italian sun.

'We were staying with one of Mum's boyfriends at his villa in the hills,' Chloe said dreamily. 'What was he called again?'

'Something really flashy like Luigi or Donatello?' said Tamsin.

'He wasn't a bloody Ninja Turtle!' Chloe shrieked. 'Wasn't he a count or something?'

Tamsin looked puzzled. 'God knows. There've been so many of them.'

'He was called Count Antonio da Silva,' said Fern, who'd never forgotten. Destiny had rolled up that long-ago summer in the form of the gardener's two teenage sons, all tanned muscles and wicked blackberry-dark eyes, who'd smoked pungent roll-ups and zoomed around on crimson scooters. Fern and Chloe had been smitten and when the boys had invited them on a visit to Pompeii they'd accepted in a heartbeat.

'We were just about to jump on their scooters when you came storming up like a paratrooper, yelling at us that we couldn't go, you miserable old cow,' Chloe reminded Tamsin.

'It was a ridiculous idea,' her sister retorted. 'Everyone knows those scooters are lethal. And I was right, as it turned out, or had you conveniently forgotten that bit?'

'Yes, yes!' Chloe flapped her hand dismissively. 'You're always right, Tamsin. Don't you ever get bored with it? But my point is that Fern was absolutely amazing! She said we weren't taking orders from anyone and then she yelled at the boys in Italian and told them to take us. Remember, Fern?'

Fern nodded. Of course she remembered. In the afternoon there'd been one of the sharp, heavy Italian downpours, the streets transformed in an instant from dusty to slick and greasy, and on the way back one of the scooters had skidded off the road. Chloe had been injured, not seriously, but still . . .

'You were almost killed, Chloe!' Tamsin interjected. 'It was bloody stupid of you both.' She fixed Fern with a beady look. '*That's* what happens when people go trying to wrestle destiny to the floor.'

'I was not almost killed! It was a sprained wrist.' Chloe giggled. 'And it was totally worth it.' She fixed wide, imploring green eyes on Fern. 'Tell her, Fern! Wasn't that magical day in Pompeii worth risking everything for?'

In Fern's memory she saw again four young people strolling through the ancient streets, felt the timeless atmosphere of the city with its sense that the citizens had only nipped out, and experienced anew the joy of holding hands with the most beautiful boy she'd ever seen. It was a bittersweet memory, though, because no experience since had ever compared to that innocent joy.

'I fell in love for the first time that day, and it was the sweetest thing imaginable,' sighed Chloe. 'The washed-out day created the most beautiful rainbow and I had my first kiss beneath it. It's still the most romantic moment of my life.'

Tamsin looked shocked. 'What, more romantic than your wedding day?'

'God, that wasn't at all romantic! It was far too

bloody stressful,' shuddered Chloe. 'The wedding night wasn't bad, though. Dom had this—'

Fern held her hands up. 'Enough detail, thanks!'

'Sorry.' Chloe grinned, looking anything but. 'Apart from my wedding night that has to be my most *innocent* romantic moment, and I'd never have had that experience if it hadn't been for Fern's devil-may-care attitude. Sometimes you just have to make things happen, otherwise you totally miss out.'

Tamsin looked as though she was about to disagree, but luckily for the harmony between the sisters the side door flew open at that point and the puppy came bounding into the kitchen, followed closely by Cybil Moss.

'Why did you have to get a puppy now?' she was complaining, her red-tipped hands flailing theatrically. 'Just when I really, really need someone to look after Petra. It's too bad of you, darling, it really is. How am I supposed to go on my cruise now?'

Tamsin rolled her eyes. 'Mummy, I'd already told you, there's no room for a Great Dane in this cottage. What's happened to her usual dog-sitter?'

Cybil's sinewy hand flew to her heart in a dramatic gesture. A veteran of countless 1970s sitcoms and adverts, she loved to use acting to her advantage, and her heavily kohled eyes widened theatrically. 'Can you believe that she's cancelled on me? At the eleventh hour?' She turned to Chloe. 'Sweetie, I don't suppose you and darling, darling Dominic would look after Petra for me? She's such an old lady now and no trouble.'

Chloe paled. 'Mum, she's the size of a Shetland pony! No way is she moving in with us. Besides, Dom's allergic to dogs.'

'Oh God, I'm undone!' Cybil wailed as she sloshed Chardonnay into a glass. 'Dimitri will take someone else on the cruise and leave me behind! My heart will break!'

Since Cybil's heart was broken on a regular basis by identikit lovers with tans so orange they could be seen from the moon and names like Raoul or Dimitri the girls were pretty used to hearing such announcements. What they weren't used to was Fern's offering to take Petra in for the week. Chloe and Tamsin goggled at their sister in astonishment and Cybil nearly dropped her wine glass on to the slate floor.

'But darling, you've never liked dogs!' Cybil exclaimed. 'You were always horribly jealous of Petra.'

'Seeing as you bought her to replace me when I

left home that's hardly surprising,' said Fern drily.

'Sibling rivalry, how sweet!' sighed Cybil. 'I love you both, silly! There's enough love for all in my heart!'

'We know,' muttered Tamsin. 'You spent our formative years proving that.'

Cybil was far too busy enfolding Fern in a Floris-scented hug to hear, but Chloe caught Fern's eye and grinned widely.

'You don't have to worry if Petra gets sick, Mum. Fern knows a great vet!'

Fern groaned. That was the only problem with having close sisters; sometimes they could read your mind. Still, it wouldn't hurt to take Petra for a check-up, would it?

Perhaps it was time she gave fate a helping hand after all.

'**P**etra's owner? The vet will see you now.'

Fern swallowed nervously. Booking an appointment for Matt to examine Petra had seemed like a really good idea yesterday, after a long phone call with Chloe and several glasses of wine, but in the cold light of day she wasn't so certain. For one thing it had been an absolute nightmare trying to squeeze a Great Dane into the Beetle and for another the surgery was overflowing with tempting pets, which was driving the huge dog wild. Hanging on to Petra was easier said than done, especially when there were lovely cats in baskets inches from her jaws. Fern was starting to think her shoulder had left its socket for good.

'Miss Moss?' The receptionist raised her voice and a note of impatience crept in. 'The vet is waiting.'

'Oh! Sorry!' Fern said, jumping from her seat and

tugging Petra up from the floor. Oh God. This was starting to feel like a very bad idea. Not only was Fern's black wrap dress covered in a thick layer of white hair but as Petra dragged her across the waiting room the red rose slide holding back her hair fell to the floor and her curls tumbled across her face, making her feel like a dead ringer for the Old English sheepdog that was next in Matt's queue.

This was *not* what she'd had in mind when she'd dressed so carefully this morning.

'At least pretend to be sick,' Fern hissed. But Petra was having a great time, bounding into the consulting room looking the perfect picture of canine health and hurling herself at Matt, whom she'd always adored.

'Hey, steady on, girl! Down!' Nearly knocked flying by the dog's enthusiastic greeting, Matt patted Petra and murmured gently to her. When he looked up at Fern, though, the expression on his face was far less welcoming, and his dark eyes were cold.

'What exactly seems to be the problem with this dog?'

Fern was taken aback. Whatever happened to *Hello, Fern, what a nice surprise to see you*? So much for that. Matt could hardly bring himself to even look at her.

'Well?'

'Petra's been staying with me while my mum's away and she's been really off her food,' she improvised wildly. 'I'm really worried. She's hardly eaten for days.'

They both looked down at the dog stretched out contentedly on the floor, flab rippling with every wag of her tail.

'Right,' said Matt coldly.

'I've asked loads of vets!' Fern fibbed. 'And they've all said they can't find anything wrong with her. But she's so old and I thought I'd better try to do something for her. Mum would never forgive me if anything happened to Petra while she was away.'

Matt said nothing but opened Petra's mouth and peered closely at her teeth before pulling a stethoscope out of his pocket and listening carefully. Then he prodded her stomach and weighed her. All the way through the examination he didn't look at Fern and the atmosphere between them was so cold she wouldn't have been surprised if a glacier had slid through the surgery.

'Maybe she's pining for Mum?' said Fern desperately. If a couple of straws had drifted past she'd have been clutching them tightly. 'Or perhaps she doesn't like Chum? Or—'

'There's absolutely nothing wrong with this dog,'

Matt snapped. 'She's overweight if anything and even if she's elderly she's in perfect health. You're completely wasting my time.'

Fern was stunned. Gentle Matt had always been laid back and easy-going. In all the time they'd been together she didn't think she'd ever heard him raise his voice.

She must have really hurt him.

Matt placed his hands on his hips and glowered at Fern. 'Are you going to tell me what the hell is going on?'

'I'm sorry,' Fern said quietly. 'I just really wanted to see you again and I wasn't sure how else to do it.'

'It's a bit late to decide you want to see me now, four years after you dumped me.' Finally Matt met her gaze and Fern saw that his eyes were glinting with anger. 'For heaven's sake, Fern, why don't you just go away and leave me alone?'

The breath caught in Fern's throat because there was no point kidding herself that his surliness meant he still had feelings for her and was still smarting from their break-up. If Matt was the one she'd let go then she'd well and truly blown it, because it seemed he couldn't stand her.

Stricken, she blinked away the tears that suddenly blurred her vision.

'I didn't mean to waste your time. I'm so sorry, Matt, this was a stupid idea. I'll go. Come on, Petra.'

But Petra wasn't listening. She was far too busy saying hello to a fluffy hamster peeping out of an unlocked cage.

'Sorry,' Fern said again, tugging on Petra's lead. 'Come on, Petra! Leave the hamster alone. She doesn't mean any harm,' she told Matt over her shoulder. 'She just wants to play.'

'I'd rather she didn't play with someone's favourite pet,' Matt snapped. 'Just hurry up and get her out, will you?'

'Petra!' gasped Fern again, yanking at the lead. 'Sorry, Matt! I'm going. Honestly!'

And she would have been too, except that once again fate decided to flip a V sign at poor Fern. She caught her foot in Petra's lead and stumbled across the room, right into a stack of cages which crashed to the floor. In the blink of an eye hamsters, gerbils and rats were scampering everywhere, noses and whiskers twitching with delight as they made a break for freedom, while the Romeo and Juliet of the white mouse world, long separated by cruel bars, took the chance to get reacquainted.

Fern lay on the floor, sawdust and sunflower seeds in her hair, and watched the ceiling spin while

Matt frantically tried to recapture the liberated rodents. God! She hoped that wasn't a rat that had just run over her stomach. She closed her eyes and groaned.

Time to apologise again. It was a shame she didn't get repeat fees.

'I'm so, so sorry,' she began, feeling like a total idiot. She opened her mouth to tell him she'd only intended to try to resolve things between them and that she never set out to wreck the surgery when she suddenly realised Matt wasn't listening.

He was far too busy laughing.

'What can possibly be funny?' Fern asked, brushing gerbil droppings from her dress. Personally she couldn't see anything to laugh about.

Matt smiled down at her and now his eyes were warm as summer rock pools with mirth. 'I'm laughing because you're like a human weapon of mass destruction! Honestly, Fern! You don't change, do you? It always was one drama after another with you. Do you remember the first time we met?'

Fern groaned. 'Of course I do!'

How could she possibly forget when that embarrassing scene was seared on her memory for life?

It had been a late September evening, the kind when the bees are drunk with nectar and the roses full blown and heavy, and Steve and Zoe had decided to throw an impromptu party to screen the first movie they'd worked on together. They'd invited a group of friends back to their flat only for the electricity to go off, leaving twenty hungry guests and no way of cooking the steaks and jacket potatoes that Zoe had prepared. The entire Victorian conversion had been plunged into darkness and Fern had no choice but to admit that her lava lamp might have been to blame. While Steve was dispatched to find fuses and failing that an electrician, Fern had taken one look at Matt's burly shoulders and frogmarched him to the nearest Homebase where they bought hurricane lamps and disposable barbecues to save the day. They'd gone on to spend the evening together in the darkness and just when Fern had felt she was going to combust with longing Matt had finally kissed some ketchup from the corner of her mouth before going in for a full smooch. At this point Steve's electrician friend had given a yell of triumph and the lights had suddenly flooded on to reveal Matt and Fern snogging in full view of everyone. It was hard to say who'd blushed more.

'That was an amazing night.' Matt looked wistful.

She gulped. He wasn't wrong. They'd gone back to his place and stayed in bed for two days, only getting up to eat or take long baths together.

'I still think about it,' he added softly. 'You were so special to me, Fern. No matter how it ended I've never regretted a second that I spent with you. I want you to know that. No matter what happens I'll never feel again the way I felt when I was with you.'

Fern felt a prickle of conscience. Should they really be having this conversation when Matt was engaged to Amanda? On the other hand, wasn't this exactly why she'd come to the surgery, to make him feel nostalgic enough to explore whether or not there was still something between them? And after all, she'd known him first, which gave her some kind of claim. Didn't it?

As Matt helped Fern to her feet and dusted her down she decided to take a chance. This was the rest of her life that was at stake here; it was no time to get cold feet.

'Matty,' Fern said before she could back out, 'I've registered Petra here and my home number's on your system now. If there's any reason why you might want to use it – any sense that maybe we have unfinished business – please call me!'

And with that she and Petra turned tail, leaving Matt and the escaped pets staring after them. Would he call? Fern wasn't certain but her heart rose with hope like a hot air balloon.

Something deep inside told her that this wasn't the last she'd be seeing of Matt.

Fern had never been the kind of girl to brood about things. She wasn't the type to mull things over, analyse the nuances of people's words or second guess their real meaning, nor did she torture herself by thinking up all the clever things she *could* have said. No, normally Fern was the type to live in the moment. But as she let herself into her flat that evening her thoughts slid back to the scene at Matt's surgery and her skin prickled with mortification. What on earth had she been thinking, turning up unannounced like that?

'You didn't help,' she said to Petra. 'If you'd left that hamster alone I might have escaped with my dignity intact.'

Heaven only knew what Matt must be thinking now. Probably what a lucky escape he'd had, thought Fern sadly. Somehow she couldn't imagine the cool and collected Amanda making a total prat of herself by tripping over and knocking cages flying. In retrospect Project Petra hadn't been such a good idea after all.

Note to self: no more planning how to get exes back when pissed.

And no more asking Chloe for advice either. Even Zoe had been taken aback when Fern had called to tell her about the disastrous visit to the vet's.

'Oh, Fern!' Zoe had sounded worried. 'That idea was hopeless from the start, I'd have thought. Matt was always so serious about his work. He'd have hated you turning up like that.'

'I know, I know,' Fern had groaned. 'I should have thought it through, but it just seemed such a good idea at the time. Chloe thought so too.'

'I bet Tamsin didn't,' Zoe had said. 'And I'm starting to wonder if I really gave you the best advice myself by encouraging you.' She'd paused for a moment. 'Maybe you should forget the whole prophecy thing, or at the very least just sit back and see what happens.'

'Hmm,' Fern had said. There was more chance of her flying to the moon than forgetting the prophecy now. It was all very well for Zoe to advise her to wait and see what unfolded when she was happily married to the love of her life. If Fern sat on her butt her soulmate could end up marrying someone else instead.

No way was she letting that happen. As far as Fern was concerned waiting was for wimps.

'After all, that psychic stuff was just a bit of fun,' Zoe had continued. 'It's probably all rubbish anyway. Maybe we should just forget it.'

'You've changed your tune!' Fern had been surprised. 'You were all for me taking fate into my own hands the other day. What's going on?' Then a thought had occurred to her. 'Is this something to do with what Angela said to you? You never did tell me exactly what that was.'

'It was really vague, that's why, and anyway it didn't really apply to my life. I just think we've been in danger of getting a bit carried away,' Zoe had replied thoughtfully. 'Besides, I know you, Fern, and I'm worried that you might do something daft.'

Like giving an engaged man my phone number, thought Fern. Maybe she wouldn't share that little detail with Zoe.

'It wouldn't be the first time, I suppose,' she'd hedged. 'Maybe you're right.'

'So you'll just wait and see? Not go off doing anything silly?'

Fern had crossed her fingers, toes and legs and anything else crossable. 'Of course not.'

'Phew!' Zoe had breathed. 'I was starting to feel really responsible for a moment there. Listen, babes, I have to dash. I'm on a night shoot in Docklands. Let's meet up soon, okay?'

And then she'd rung off, leaving Fern feeling guilty because she had absolutely no intention of leaving something as important as finding her soulmate to chance. As if.

But what Zoe didn't know wouldn't upset her, right?

With a heavy sigh Fern shoved some bread under the grill to toast, forked dog food into Petra's bowl and then made herself a cup of coffee so strong that the spoon practically stood up and waved at her. While she waited for the toast she checked the messages on her answerphone, her heart sinking because all three were from Seb. Not that this came as a surprise. Since Zoe's wedding he'd taken to leaving long regretful messages in which he apologised repeatedly and told her how much he loved her. Deleting each one without listening to it Fern felt her appetite vanish. No matter how many times Freda or Zoe gave her a pep talk she couldn't help feeling guilty because Seb sounded so sorry and so sad. Maybe she should forgive him? Everyone made mistakes after all; it didn't necessarily make them a bad person. I treated Matt really badly, Fern told herself, and I'm not a horrible person. And in her heart she knew that neither was Seb, deep down.

Okay. Make that very, very deep down.

Should she call him? For a second Fern's fingers hovered over the telephone as she toyed with the idea. It would be so easy to pick up where they'd left off. She could move back into the spacious Docklands apartment, be part of a couple again, and on the surface everything would be lovely. But underneath there'd be the choking weeds of her resentment, which even though she could try to ignore them would surely pull her under, for how could she bear to let Seb touch her while knowing he'd been with Vanessa? And how would she ever be able to trust him again?

Fern's hand fell away from the phone. There was no way she could make that call however much she might wish she could. Sometimes the clock just couldn't be turned back.

Picking up her mug of coffee, she wandered into her sitting room. A long solitary evening stretched ahead, and as she flicked through the satellite channels she started to feel really low. Had all her life choices really led to this, being all alone with nothing but an elderly dog and Sky Plus to keep her company? If she'd known she'd end up feeling like this at thirty-one, Fern thought, she would have done things very differently. Would she have thrown Matt away so carelessly?

'Of course I wouldn't,' she said to Petra and her voice felt tight with tears. 'What if I've really screwed everything up?'

But Petra was asleep, no doubt dreaming lovely doggy dreams about chasing hamsters, and her only reply was a low rumbling snore. Resigning herself to a quiet evening in, Fern curled up beneath her heavy crimson chenille throw and leaned her head back against the cushions. Perhaps she'd just close her eyes for a minute . . .

Beep! Beep! Beep! Beep!

The loud shrilling of the smoke alarm almost sent Fern into orbit and caused her heart to drum against her ribs. The sitting room was thick with smoke and no sooner had she opened her eyes than they were streaming. Petra was barking loudly and running to and from the kitchen, her huge tail knocking the cold coffee flying.

'Shit! The toast!' gasped Fern, tearing into the

kitchen, where thick black smoke was billowing from the charcoaled remains of her supper. Turning off the grill and flinging open the back door she took some big gulps of air before retrieving the toast and tossing it out on to the lawn. Barking, Petra galloped into the darkness after it. Fern clambered up on to the table to reach the reset button on the smoke alarm but without platform boots her fingers were inches away.

'Bloody, bloody hell!' she swore. 'What else can possibly go wrong today?'

She must have done something seriously horrific in a past life to be attracting all this bad luck. Close to tears with frustration she inched her way down from the table and started to search for her boots, which was easier said than done in the dense smoke.

'Fern? Are you all right, dear?' Freda appeared at the back door. 'I heard the alarm and hopped over the wall. Is there a fire? Shall I call the fire brigade?'

'I burned my toast,' Fern explained, in between coughing fits. 'But it's all under control now.'

'Really?' Freda looked dubiously at the billowing smoke. 'Gracious, that alarm's loud. Can't you turn it off?'

'It's too high, Free. I can't reach it!'

'Hang on, I'll do it.' With an agility that belied

her sixty-three years Freda climbed on to the table and stretched up to silence the alarm. The relief of having the harsh sound silenced made Fern feel giddy.

'Come outside and get your breath,' Freda ordered, taking Fern's arm and guiding her out into the garden. They sat side by side on the low brick wall and Fern took some deep gulps of cool air until slowly but surely her breathing came under control, although her eyes still smarted and the back of her throat felt raw.

'Whatever happened?' asked Freda.

Fern groaned. 'I'm such an idiot. I must have nodded off while the toast was cooking. I could have burned the house down.'

'Nonsense!' Freda said briskly. 'Of course you couldn't, love. That's what smoke alarms are for. Thank goodness you had one.'

'I can't take the credit, I'm afraid. Tamsin got it for me.'

'Well, hurray for Tamsin then.' Freda sniffed the air. 'Goodness, but that smoky smell brings back memories.' Her eyes took on a faraway expression. 'There was this small café in Jerusalem where the air was always heavy with smoke. The men used to sit around with their hubble-bubble pipes scented with apple and other rather exotic substances. They were certainly taken aback when I asked to have a go.'

Fern loved it when her neighbour reminisced about her travels. Freda's adventures were exactly the kind of excitement she'd longed for when she'd been feeling so tied down by Matt. She'd had her own adventures when she'd left him to travel through Asia and those memories would last for ever, but lately she had started to wonder whether she'd made the right decision.

'Only you can answer that question,' said Freda when Fern pondered this aloud.

'But is that how it has to be?' Fern stared up at the dark sky, sprinkled with stars like glitter on a Christmas card, and felt very lonely. 'Do you really have to sacrifice freedom for love? Is it really one or the other? Can't you have both?'

The older woman shrugged. 'I don't have the answer to that, my love. I'm hardly an expert on relationships, am I?'

'You can't tell me you've never been in love.'

Freda sighed. 'Oh, I've been in love all right, girly. Not that it made me very happy.'

Fern said nothing. Freda was very secretive about her love life but Fern had long suspected that the core of cynicism hid a deep sadness. As the darkness wrapped itself around them she felt her skin grow warm with anticipation as Freda began to describe her travels through Australia and how she'd stopped in Sydney to take a teaching job for six months.

'I really thought I was beyond all that soppy romance stuff, above it even, so when I met Greg I was taken aback by how he made me feel.' She smiled ruefully. 'Every cliché under the sun, I felt it! He taught science but his passion was sailing and most evenings he would take a boat out across the bay. One evening he invited me to join him and it was amazing! I'd never seen anyone so vital and so alive.'

Freda paused, in her memories no longer an ageing woman with grey hair but a young girl again with soft unlined skin and long dark curls who'd made love to her sailor beneath the bright Antipodean stars.

'We were together for two years,' she continued. 'One Christmas we sailed up the western coast together and it was the most amazing, magical time. I didn't think it was possible to be so in love, or so happy.'

'What happened?' breathed Fern. Freda was devoted to the single life so she knew this story didn't end with wedding bells.

Freda twisted her hands in her lap. 'Halfway

through that trip I got a message from England to say that my father was seriously ill. I asked Greg to fly home with me but his heart was set on going on so I came back alone.' She swallowed. 'I never saw him again. By the time I returned to Sydney he'd taken up the offer of a place on the America's Cup team and was miles away.'

'Bastard!'

Freda shook her head. 'Greg pursued his dreams. He chose freedom over love and for him it must have been the right thing. He returned to Sydney, or so I heard through mutual friends, but I'd moved on by then. He married shortly after that, I believe, and I hope he's been very happy.' She smiled wistfully. 'I've never forgotten him. In fact, not a day goes by when I don't think about what might have been if I hadn't had to fly back to the UK. I guess I've always thought of Greg as the one who got away.'

Fern stared at her neighbour, aghast. Would this be her thirty years from now?

'Anyway, that's enough of my maudlin wittering on! What would I know anyway about love?' Visibly collecting herself, Freda smoothed her creased skirt and checked her watch. 'Gracious! I'll be late for bridge at this rate. Now are you sure you're going to be all right? You're looking very pale.'

If Fern looked pale it was nothing to do with almost burning her house down. That hardly compared to a lifetime without the love of her life, did it?

Reassuring her neighbour that she was fine, Fern kissed Freda's soft powdery cheek and thanked her once again for her help. Then Freda clambered back over the low wall and Fern returned to her kitchen. The smell of smoke still lingered a little so she sprayed Oust liberally round the flat and opened a few more windows before she set about cleaning the grill pan, scrubbing and scouring as though her life depended on it. Anything was better than thinking about Freda's story and dwelling on the possible parallels with her own situation. Her pulse quickened with rising panic.

When the phone rang Fern pounced on it. Chatting to someone, anyone, even Seb, had to be better than driving herself crackers with endless questions and what ifs. If it was Tamsin she could thank her for the smoke alarm and if it was Zoe she'd tell the story in such a way that they'd soon be howling with laughter. Even if it was Cybil calling to check on Petra Fern would be pleased to hear from her.

But the caller wasn't any of these.

'Fern?' The voice, low and throbbing with emotion, was so unexpected that her knees turned to water. 'It's me, Matt. I've been thinking all day about what you said and you're right, there is unfinished business between us. Can I see you?'

Fern slithered down against the cooker and sat on the sticky kitchen floor. Her mouth was suddenly dry.

'Fern?' Matt said. 'Is that okay? Can I come over?'

This was it, Fern told herself; this was her opportunity to take her future in both hands. If she didn't then what was to say that in thirty years' time she wouldn't be as filled with regrets as her neighbour? She couldn't bear that.

So there was really only one answer.

'Oh, Matt.' Her heart broke into a gallop. 'Do you really need to ask? Of course you can come over. Come as quickly as you can.'

11

When Matt rang off Fern tore around the flat like a small blonde version of the Tasmanian Devil, sweeping magazines and newspapers under the sofa, plumping cushions and hurling washing up into the dishwasher. The Jo Malone basil and lime scented candle flickering in the fireplace chased away the last traces of smoke and the table lamps threw pools of warm yellow light across the room. There was no time to do much about her own dishevelled appearance so she just swapped her smoky dress for a pair of wide-legged trousers and a cream, angel-sleeved top, pinned her unruly curls up with a glittery clip and dabbed her favourite Benefit perfume behind her ears. She didn't want to look as though she'd made too much effort.

Actually, Fern wasn't quite sure *what* she wanted from this visit, but at least she could look presentable and be in a reasonably tidy flat while she decided. Matt had always been a neatness freak – Fern's constant mess and disorganisation had driven him crackers – so it would be nice to impress him with how she'd changed during the time since they'd broken up.

Okay, thought Fern as she hid the ironing pile under the sink, maybe she hadn't changed quite as much as she would have liked, but she'd thought about being more tidy and it was the thought that counted, wasn't it?

She was just contemplating doing battle with the Hoover when there was a loud knock at the door. Petra hurtled past Fern into the hall and began to bark loudly, only stopping when Matt spoke to her through the letter box.

'Petra, it's me. Good girl. Let me in, Fern, it's started pouring out here!'

'Petra! Shush!' Grabbing the dog's collar Fern hauled her away from the door. 'Sorry,' she called as she unlocked the Chubb. 'I think Petra has delusions that she's a guard dog.'

'Some guard dog,' said Matt wryly as Petra rolled over and offered up her tummy to be tickled. 'Wish I had this effect on every girl I meet!'

Fern wasn't sure what to say to this. She could

always do the same, she supposed, but poor old Matt would probably die of shock.

'It's nice to see your flat.' Matt straightened up and smiled at Fern. 'I was trying to picture where you live.'

'Well, here it is!' Fern said brightly. 'It's little and cramped but it's home.'

Matt looked around at the narrow hall with its pink fairy lights, bright splashy paintings and rainbow rug and nodded. 'It's very you.'

It was, and Matt seemed enormous in it. His tall frame filled the narrow hallway and rain drops from his Barbour pooled on the laminate. Suddenly Fern's nerves were jangling so loudly she was surprised Matt couldn't hear them. Being alone in her flat with him felt really odd and strangely clandestine.

'Would you like a drink?' she asked, surprised at just how on edge she was feeling. 'Tea? Coffee? Diet Coke?'

'Fern,' said Matt softly, 'stop wittering on about drinks. I think we both know this isn't just a social visit.'

Fern swallowed. Matt's eyes, the lashes still spiky from the rain, were smoky with passion. When he pulled her hard against him and kissed her his mouth echoed that emotion while his fingers threaded through her curls, pulling her closer and closer. He kissed Fern like a drowning man gulping air before abruptly pushing her away.

'Christ!' He stared at her, aghast. 'I didn't mean to do that.'

Fern sagged against the wall, her legs turned to boiled string by the intensity of his kiss. In all the time they'd been a couple he'd never kissed her like that. What the hell was going on?

'So why did you then?' she whispered.

'I couldn't *not* kiss you!' Matt grated. A muscle ticked in his left cheek, an old indication of tension. 'For God's sake, Fern! What are you trying to do to me?'

'I'm not trying to do anything!' But even before the words left her lips Fern knew deep down that it wasn't true. From the minute she'd seen Matt at Zoe's wedding she'd been wondering if he was the soulmate she'd let go and whether he still had feelings for her.

Well, that was no longer in question. There were clearly very strong feelings on his side, and from the way her heart was ricocheting against her ribcage she wasn't immune herself.

Matt gave her a rueful look. 'You sought *me* out, remember? And what extraordinary lengths you went to, tracking down my practice and inventing an illness for your mother's dog.'

Fern's cheeks flamed. Thank goodness Matt didn't know she'd offered to take charge of Petra just for that very purpose. He'd think she was a stalker or something.

Actually, the way he'd put it even *she* was starting to think she was a stalker.

'And then,' he continued, folding his arms and staring down at her, 'you deliberately registered Petra with me and left your details there, knowing that I couldn't possibly ignore them. You knew exactly what you were doing, Fern.'

'Okay! Guilty as charged!' Fern held up her hands. 'But I didn't make you jump in your car and drive here to see me, did I? That was your decision, Matty, and no one else's.'

'But you know how I felt about you.' Matt sighed. 'It was never a secret, was it, Fern? I thought I'd always let you know how I felt, showed you I loved you and treated you right. Surely you must have known?'

She hung her head. Of course she'd known. In all their time together Matt had never let her down. Why hadn't she had the sense to see something good when it was right under her nose?

'I loved you so much, Fern,' Matt continued, his eyes still dark with emotion as he stared at her across the hallway. 'Christ, I was going to ask you to marry me, that's how strongly I felt about you. I really thought you loved me and that we were going to make it.' He gave a harsh laugh. 'Well, how bloody wrong can a man be? While I was planning the future you must have been frantically planning your escape. Did you laugh about it while you were travelling through Asia? Or were you too busy thanking your lucky stars that you'd escaped?'

Fern stared at him, horrified. 'Of course not! I had no idea you were contemplating getting married!'

'Of course you didn't.' Matt ran his hands through his sooty hair, making clumps stand up in outrage. 'I didn't even figure in your plans, did I?'

'That's not true!'

'And then, just when I get my life together, just when I've met someone who's really good for me and actually wants to be with me, you decide it's a good idea to revisit the past!' Matt shook his head. 'Your timing's bloody fantastic, isn't it? And here I am like some pathetic schoolboy because, even when I hated you, Fern, and believe me there was a time when I *really* hated you, I never stopped loving you too. And it might be a cliché but do you know what? There's never been a day that's gone by when I haven't thought about you and wondered *what if*?'

He paused and the silence between them grew like a living presence. Then the fight seemed to seep out of Matt and his shoulders slumped.

'Why did you leave like that, Fern? I've always wondered. Was it something I did wrong or did you just not love me enough?'

'I was scared,' Fern whispered. 'You were getting so serious, Matt, and I just didn't feel ready for all that. I was frightened.'

'Frightened?' he echoed incredulously. 'What the hell for? We were really good together.'

'I was scared of how serious we were becoming.' Fern closed her eyes. When couples got serious there was a strong chance they got hurt, in her experience, and if someone you really loved left you it took a long time, if ever, to recover. She'd loved her father and losing him had been bad enough. What would it be like to lose a soulmate? The answer could only be unbearable. Her mother had never recovered from losing Roger and Fern hadn't been sure that she could handle that kind of heartache again. She hadn't been able to articulate these thoughts at the time but now, standing in her cramped hallway on a rainy evening, she finally understood why she'd run away from Matt. It wasn't because she hadn't loved him. It was because she'd been afraid of getting hurt.

The irony was that she'd only succeeded in hurting them both.

Matt, who wasn't party to this sudden epiphany, was still brimful of several years' worth of anger and determined to have his say. 'People get serious, Fern, when they fall in love; that's what happens in adult relationships. But you.' He frowned. 'You seem to spend your whole time running away from anything that looks remotely like commitment.'

There wasn't much that Fern could say to this because Matt had a point. Maybe that was why she'd chosen Seb, who wouldn't recognise commitment if it ran up and kneed him in the groin.

'I didn't mean to hurt you,' she said softly. 'And if it's any consolation I really regret how I treated you. It's not something I'm proud of.'

'Well, you did hurt me and it's taken me a long time to get over it. But it's ancient history now, right?' Matt said angrily. 'I'm with someone else and my life's moved on. We're nothing to each other now, Fern, which is exactly what you wanted.'

Fern said nothing. If he was going to have a go at her it was probably the least she deserved for leaving him in such a cowardly way. She bit down on her bottom lip and mentally prepared herself for a tongue-lashing.

But it never happened. Instead Matt exhaled heavily. 'Who am I trying to fool? There's probably a part of me that's never got over it and still hates you for what you did, but I guess deep down I've always known you didn't mean to be cruel.' He stepped forward and took her trembling hands in his. 'But you do need to stop running away, Fern, and always thinking that a serious relationship ties you down when the reality is that being loved sets you free and gives you the strength to be yourself. We had something really special once, you know. We could have been really good together.'

Fern looked up into his eyes, dark Bournville chocolate irises delicately ringed with black as though drawn by a painstaking artist, and her heart skipped a beat. There was still love in those eyes, wasn't there?

'Maybe we still could be,' she whispered. 'It isn't too late, is it?'

Matt sighed wearily. 'God, Fern. I don't know. Things have changed, haven't they? Besides, I'm engaged to Amanda and she's a good person. She doesn't deserve to be let down.'

'Sorry, of course she doesn't.' Guilt-stricken, Fern tried to pull her hands away but Matt's grip only tightened.

'Hell, I already feel I'm betraying Amanda in my mind at least a thousand times a day with thoughts of you and what could have been. But now? Hell, do you think we met up again for a reason?' Matt ran his hand through his thick dark hair. 'I don't know what to do here. How can I possibly marry another woman if I've still got feelings for someone else?'

Fern could see how anguished Matt was, and it tore her up inside. She took a sharp breath. 'You still have feelings for me?'

'Jesus, Fern, you have no idea!' Matt stepped forward and wound his arms round her, pulling her so close to his chest that she could feel his racing heartbeat. 'I've imagined seeing you again for so long – I was going to tell you how angry I was with you but now it's actually happening all I want to do is hold you and kiss you!'

Fern was totally lost for words. This angry, passionate man wasn't the steady, reliable guy she remembered. Matt was always so honest, so true to his word. No wonder he was in turmoil. These feelings were completely contrary to his nature. There surely had to be something between them still? She felt a thrill of excitement. The man she remembered as almost staid and set in his ways, who only liked to make love on Sunday mornings and whose idea of an exciting night out was a trip to Pizza Express, *was* capable of throwing caution to the wind after all.

So maybe it was time she let him.

Then Matt was kissing her again, his mouth iron hard on hers and his tongue urgently exploring the softness of her lips. So maybe it was a little like a washing machine on spin cycle and perhaps the hands grasping her buttocks and skimming her nipples were a little desperate? These things didn't matter, Fern told herself sternly, not if Matt was her soulmate. If he was a little heavy-handed it was only because he was so consumed with passion, right? Throwing caution to the wind Fern kissed Matt back and gasped when his hands strayed beneath her top, his fingers tracing patterns across her tummy and back before moving to her breasts . . .

'Oh God, Fern,' Matt groaned, his lip grazing her throat. 'I've never stopped thinking about you.'

'I can tell,' Fern gasped. Since when had Matt become so commanding? When they were together he couldn't even decide what to have for dinner – it had driven her crazy – but now he was playing pass the parcel with their clothes and making her giddy with the delicious sensations rippling through her body. At this rate they wouldn't even make it to the bedroom. Plucking his T-shirt from the waistband of his jeans and sliding her hands beneath, Fern cried out in surprise. Since when did Matt have a physique that would make Peter Andre weep with envy? Where had those amazing abs come from?

'I joined a gym when you left.' Matt laughed, seeing Fern's stunned expression. 'I didn't have a lot else to do with myself and after a few weeks of comfort eating I knew I had to do something. I never thought I'd say it, but I'm actually a bit of an exercise junkie these days.'

Fern couldn't have been more amazed if Matt had told her he split atoms in his spare time. The Matt she remembered had been the ultimate couch potato. All he'd wanted to do was cuddle up on the sofa to watch a DVD and scoff a Chinese. His idea of exercise had been picking up the remote control. She ran her fingers over his newly honed physique. His skin was honey hued and warm beneath her touch and very, very smooth.

Wait a minute. Had he waxed his chest? Surely he hadn't always been this hairless. This was Matt, but at the same time it wasn't *her* Matt. This was a new Matt.

Amanda's Matt.

While Fern wrestled with this uncomfortable thought the tinny tone of Matt's mobile split the charged atmosphere. Unhooking it from his belt, Matt frowned.

'I have to take this call.'

Part of her was aching with desire while the other part was almost relieved. Pushing her hair away from her flushed cheeks she moved into the sitting room, with its candles and lamplight, and left Matt to his call. She didn't intend to listen – after all there were only so many times a girl could pretend to be interested in the finer points of a calving – but when she heard him snap, 'Stop panicking and listen, Amanda!' her ears pricked up.

''Manda, listen to me. You won't be able to wait for David to assist. You'll have to do this one on your own,' Matt was saying. 'Of course you can! I'll talk you through it. Yes, plenty of jelly. Just reach in. Can you feel the legs?'

Eurgh! Fern felt faint. She couldn't even watch *Holby City* without needing fresh air, but Amanda could reach inside cows and turn their calves round? That was awesome stuff. She inched closer to the door and tuned in to what was turning out to be better than *The Archers*.

Not that Fern would ever admit that she listened to *The Archers*. She kept her guilty Radio 4 habit to herself.

'Okay, sweetheart, that sounds great,' Matt said warmly. 'Now ease the calf out, very slowly. Break the membrane and apply suction to the nostrils to clear the mucus. No, the blood is the mother's, I'd say.'

Enough detail already. Feeling queasy, Fern retreated to the sofa, tucking her top back in and smoothing her hair down. The talk of blood and mucus had well and truly broken the mood. A few minutes later she heard Matt ring off with a muttered, 'Yeah, me too,' and snap his phone shut. Guilt knotted Fern's stomach. What was she doing? Matt was *engaged*, for heaven's sake!

'Sorry, Fern, but I needed to take that call.' Matt hovered in the doorway between the sitting room and the hallway.

'That was Amanda, right? She's a vet too?'

He nodded. 'She works in Hampshire. It's a rural practice and a bit more cutting edge than tending to poodles and hamsters in Putney.'

'You always did want to practise in the country,' Fern recalled. Matt loved rural life whereas she felt twitchy if she was more than five minutes from Pret a Manger.

'I still do,' Matt said. 'I'll do a few more years in London and then the plan is for us to look out for a partnership somewhere rural. Somerset appeals.' He stood there, wavering. 'I'm sorry, Fern, but I can't do this, not while I'm with someone else. It just feels wrong.'

'I know, Matt. To me too. Perhaps you should leave.'

'Perhaps I should.' But still he remained hovering in the hallway, and Fern remained glued to the sofa. Wasn't she as bad as Vanessa right now? Worse, even. There was no way that Fern wanted to put another woman through that kind of heartbreak, no matter how much she wanted to let Matt kiss her until she turned to mush.

'Fern, I need some time to think about everything that's happened here this evening. I swear I didn't plan any of this. Amanda is wonderful, and she wants the same things in life as me. And then there's you, so flamboyant and sexy. Amanda doesn't deserve to be hurt in this way, but should I call the engagement off if I feel so strongly about you?' At the rate he was running his fingers through his hair, he might not have any left by the end of this visit. 'Oh, hell, I don't know what the right thing is to do.'

Matt was so honest that this really shouldn't have surprised Fern. Of course he'd want to do the right thing. Matt, unlike some people she could think of, wouldn't cheat on his partner for months on end and Fern wouldn't want him to, but to break his engagement off so swiftly? That was major stuff, and not to be done on a whim!

'Can I call you when I've got my head on straight?'

Fern nodded, not meeting his eyes. Matt was such a good guy. Back when they were dating he often described the idyllic life he had in mind where people cooked on Agas, stomped through mud with their retrievers and drove about in battered Land Rover Defenders. Waitrose, smart boutiques and theatre didn't seem to figure in the equation at all.

But maybe it was time that she grew up. Her sisters seemed blissfully happy with their rural lives and even Zoe had been talking about moving out of the city now that she was married. Perhaps this was what grown-up women in their thirties actually did. Was it time to embrace her inner Boden catalogue? She'd have to work really hard on liking mud and bracing walks, maybe take out a subscription to *Country Living* and buy herself a pair of funky flowery wellies or something. Suddenly all Fern's old fears and niggles about their compatibility started nipping at her like red ants.

'Hey,' said Matt gently, placing his forefinger beneath Fern's chin and tilting her face upwards in order to smile down into her eyes, 'you okay?'

She swallowed. The sensation of his strong fingers against her skin made her shiver and for a second she was transported right back to their first ever kiss. The old feelings were still there, stretching and yawning as they came back to life. Matt made her feel safe and loved and she wanted nothing more than to push her scruples aside, take his hand and lead him into her bedroom, but something was stopping her.

It was all too much too fast.

'I don't want you to rush into anything,' she told him firmly. 'There's no pressure and certainly no expectations on my part, Matt, and please don't make any hasty decisions because of me. If you don't want to be with Amanda it should be because you don't feel right about committing to her, not because you're wondering what could have been between us. Are you sure that you're not getting confused here?'

Matt laughed. 'Is that the end of the sermon? And anyway, how did you get so wise?'

'Bitter experience mostly. Seriously, Matty. I

want you to have a really hard think about all this. Don't do anything you may regret, okay? And,' she turned her head swiftly so that his kiss fell on the corner of her mouth, 'that includes kissing me.'

Matt looked as though he was about to argue but then his mobile rang and distracted him from what he was about to say. Minutes later he flipped it shut with a grimace of annoyance.

'Bad news?' Fern asked. She couldn't help thinking there was something very sexy about Matt when he went into serious vet mode.

'There's an emergency at work. I need to get back to the surgery straight away and operate. My locum is in a real state so I'll have to dash. But I'll call you, okay?'

'Okay,' Fern told him, standing on tiptoes to kiss him goodbye, her bones melting with tenderness when his soft lips brushed hers and his strong arms clasped her close to that newly honed chest. Then he was gone, striding through the garden and swallowed up by the darkness. Once his Discovery had roared into life and growled away down the street Fern shut the front door and leaned against it, feeling weak from a strange cocktail of relief and disappointment that he'd had to leave.

Was Matt the one after all? Was there hope for

them? Fern touched her lips which were still tingling from his kisses and felt excitement bubble up inside her. If this was taking fate into her own hands then she was all for it!

12

'This is a great party!' Fern's trainee Kim exclaimed. 'I'm so glad we came, aren't you?'

'Mmm,' mumbled Fern into her glass of champagne. To be honest she was starting to doubt the wisdom of coming to this Movie Legends costume party, but nineteen-year-old Kim was all sparkly-eyed with excitement and it seemed mean to dampen her enthusiasm. Besides, their boss Jeremy had bought the tickets and insisted that his team had a night out on the tiles.

'Come on, girlfriend!' he'd wailed when Fern had tried to make her excuses. 'We haven't been out for *ages*! You're getting old before your time. You can't stay in watching soaps and eating Marks and Spencer's meals for one for ever!'

'I'm not doing that,' Fern had snapped, stung by the implication that since Seb's departure she'd had less of a social life than a hermit.

Jeremy had raised a quizzical eyebrow. 'Oh really? Then how come none of us have seen you lately?'

'Because I've been busy!' Fern had retorted and her boss had shrugged. He'd worked with Fern long enough to know when to leave a subject alone. Besides, his work was already done. There was enough truth in his words to needle Fern and a rather worrying collection of ready meals for one in her freezer set the alarm bells ringing. Maybe, she'd thought as she sketched out a set for a new production of *Cymbeline*, it was time she started socialising again.

Two weeks had passed since Matt's unexpected visit, fourteen days during which Fern had leapt into orbit each time her phone rang only to come crashing back down to earth when it wasn't him. Matt, it appeared, was having a long hard think.

Several times her finger had hovered over the call button on the key pad but something had stopped her from being the one to initiate contact. Was Matt embarrassed about his out-of-character behaviour? Or perhaps in the cold light of day he'd realised that a calf-delivering, animal-loving fiancée was exactly what he needed rather than a scatty townie who loved platform boots and shopping? He was engaged, too, Fern reminded herself sharply. Amanda was the woman he'd decided to spend the rest of his life with, and for a guy like Matt that wasn't a decision that would have been made lightly. He must love Amanda, so maybe that evening with Fern had just been an attack of cold feet, a last trip down memory lane before forsaking all others for ever?

Yes, that was it. She'd clearly made a complete fool of herself, and he'd run straight back into calm, sane Amanda's arms, shell-shocked from his encounter with a crazy ex.

So here she was in a hot, crowded bar in the Docklands, surrounded by movie icons and excited colleagues, drinking white wine so rough that her mouth was going furry and already missing her comfy sofa and lasagne for one.

Oh dear. Maybe Jeremy had a point and she *was* old before her time?

'There's loads of well fit guys, too!' Kim's bright eyes were out on stalks. 'I think we've beaten the odds in the London dating universe, Fern!'

Fern grimaced. Kim's beer goggles were already in place. Looking round the room she could see two reasonably cute guys at a push. 'Yeah, right,' she said.

Kim dug her bony elbow into Fern's ribs. 'Oh come on, Fern, have some fun. Or are you past it now you're over thirty?'

Fern didn't dignify this with a reply, but feeling about a hundred she glanced down at her watch and tried to estimate how long she ought to wait before she could make a swift exit.

'I'm going to talk to that Charlie Chaplin; he's got a really cute bum!' Kim decided, draining her drink and running her hands through her long dark hair. 'See you later. Much later, with any luck!' and she darted away through the press of bodies in the direction of her prey.

Fern sighed and wished she had even an ounce of the younger girl's enthusiasm. It was the first time she'd been out socialising since Zoe's wedding, if you discounted visits to the vet, and she really ought to make more of an effort.

Maybe it was time she forgot the whole damn prophecy business. After all, it hadn't made her very happy so far. Sod Matt. Would she have thought of him if she hadn't been prompted by the reading? There were plenty more fish in the sea.

Never one to look a gift horse in the mouth she took another glass of champagne and glanced around the room. It was time to prove that the whole mystic business was total and utter nonsense. Spotting a gorgeous blond guy in a gorilla suit who'd just taken his costume head off to drink, she straightened her wig, took a deep breath and prepared herself for a conversation with King Kong.

'Is it okay if I sit here for a moment and catch my breath?' she asked, gesturing towards the empty seat beside him.

'Be my guest. I promise I won't snatch you up and scale a skyscraper!' King Kong's navy blue eyes sparkled. 'Hey, you've come as *Thoroughly Modern Millie*! That's one of my all-time favourite films!'

'It is?' Delighted to be recognised – Kim hadn't even heard of the film – Fern took this as a good omen and slipped into the seat. 'I really love *King Kong*!'

Gorilla man pulled a face. 'It's not a great choice – I'm melting here! Still, it was all I could find at short notice.' He held out a hand. 'I'm Pete, by the way, when I'm not being Kong!'

Fern laughed and shook his hand. 'I'm Fern!'

As they sipped their drinks and chatted Fern found herself beginning to relax. Pete was great company and really easy to talk to. Although they worked for the same company Pete was based in accounts so their paths hadn't crossed before.

Several drinks later they were bantering away like old friends and Pete was telling Fern how much he hated his job.

'Lucky you working on the creative side,' he sighed. 'I'm so bored in accounts. The department is totally mismanaged, too. If they'd only let me have some autonomy I know I could turn it round.'

'Poor you,' said Fern. She didn't have a clue about accounts – the haphazard state of her current account proved that – but she'd had several drinks and it was nice to have the undivided attention of a good-looking man. Pete was a gentleman, too, she thought as she sipped her champagne. He'd not made any moves and seemed genuinely interested in her life and career. It was only fair that she listened to him in turn.

But the more he talked the more morose he became, staring into his pint glass with a maudlin expression on his face. Fern tried to cheer him up by moaning a bit about her own job and life in general, and he did start to smile when she described how Petra had created havoc at the vet's. She drew the line at telling him why she was there, though. She wanted to keep her remaining shreds of dignity.

She was just telling him about Alek's offer of a job in Prague and how tempted she was when several of his colleagues appeared and dragged him protesting on to the dance floor. Laughing at the spectacle of a gorilla trying to do the macarena Fern rejoined Jeremy and Kim. She'd catch Pete later, she decided as she accepted another glass of champagne from her boss. He seemed like a nice guy, so who knew what might happen?

'Hey, Fern,' Kim shrilled as Fern appeared at her elbow. 'There you are. This is Sam. He was just saying how much he liked the set we did for *Jane*. I told him it was all your work!'

Fern looked up and then up some more. The man Kim had towed across the room had to be at least six feet tall and his black Darth Vader costume added to the impression of height. Thick locks of chestnut hair fell across his face, almost but not quite hiding merry hazel eyes and a wide curly mouth. She had a sudden urge to go over to the dark side.

'I'm glad you liked *Jane*.' Fern smiled up at him, thinking what a sweet face he had. Her gaze slid down to his left hand where the fingers were ring-free. Wow. Two attractive single guys at the same party; that surely had to contravene some law of physics.

'I loved it,' Sam told her warmly. 'I work in a similar line for Carlton. Maybe we ought to poach you?'

'Don't you dare,' Jeremy warned. 'She's our secret weapon.'

Fern laughed. 'Some weapon! Though come to think of it someone told me only recently that I'm a human WMD. Don't worry, Jerry, I'm not going anywhere.'

'Not even on to the dance floor?' Sam asked, holding out his hand. 'I'm sure I could persuade you to defect once you've seen my moves.'

Fern fanned her face. 'I'm far too hot to dance. I think I need some air.'

'How about the balcony? We can chat out there. It's much cooler and quieter.'

Nodding agreement, Fern followed him through the dancing partygoers towards the French windows at the end of the room.

'That's better,' Sam said, sliding across one of the glass windows and leading her on to a balcony terrace. 'It's much cooler out here.'

'What an amazing view,' Fern gasped, leaning against the wrought-iron balustrade and peering down into the inky Thames. Beyond glittered the city, diamond lights against velvet blackness with the sparkling ring of the London Eye winking across the water. She'd never get used to living in the capital; she loved the thrum of life and the tangible excitement that crackled in the atmosphere. It proved, as if she needed any more proof, just how unsuited she and Matt really had been.

Fern and Sam leaned on the balcony side by side and watched the churning river. A party boat cruised by, fairy lights scattering rubies and emeralds across the water, and the sound of chatter drifting on the breeze. They gossiped for a while about work, laughing when they realised they had ex-colleagues in common, and sipped at their drinks while the Thames slithered past. Fern felt herself relax. Sam was funny, attentive and very definitely flirting with her.

As her vision started to sway a little she began to realise just how much she'd had to drink. Not enough to make her rolling drunk, but enough to take the edge off her nerves and buoy up her confidence. She was also suddenly aware of how close she was standing to Sam, close enough to catch the scent of his aftershave on the night breeze and feel his forearm brush hers as they leaned over the iron balustrade. Suddenly her heart was racing and she ached for him to touch her. Feeling brave, she placed her hand on Sam's chest where sure enough his heart was galloping too.

'Your heart's racing,' she whispered.

Sam's lips grazed her temple. 'That's because I'm all alone with the most beautiful girl in London. Fern, can I kiss you?'

It was such a romantic setting. The stars were silver embroidery on a black velvet sky and the slice of moon was as sweet and shy as Sam's smile. *Why not?* She raised her face up to his. Angela's words about soulmates had been nothing but nonsense.

'I'd really like that,' she murmured.

Sam's kiss was soft and gentle, a butterfly's wings skimming across her lips. Fern closed her eyes and savoured the feeling of his strong arms round her own slender shoulders as he held her close against his chest. Bubbles of desire popped through her bloodstream as she kissed him back, her tongue dancing with his as his mouth became more demanding.

Sam tasted so delicious. Of minty toothpaste, a hint of Stella Artois, and salt . . .

Hang on a minute. Salt?

Fern's eyes snapped open and to her horror she realised that Sam was crying. And not with joy either, because he broke their embrace off abruptly, mumbling, 'I'm sorry, I can't do this. I just can't!'

Fern was aghast. Maybe she should just give up with relationships if this was the effect she had on men. First Matt and now Sam! Even Pete had gone missing, just when she'd thought things looked promising.

'Sam? Whatever's the matter? Did I do something wrong?'

Sam had turned his back on her. His big frame was racked with silent sobs, his strong shoulders rising and falling in time with each angry choking gasp. Tentatively Fern put a hand on his shoulder blade. She couldn't bear to see such distress.

'Sam? Please! Can't you tell me what's wrong?'

'Oh God, Fern, I'm so sorry. This isn't your fault,' he choked. He dashed a hand across his eyes, impatiently trying to scrub away his tears. 'Christ, I'm a disaster, even now. After all this time!'

Perplexed, Fern patted his back and murmured gently, as though comforting one of her nieces. Slowly Sam's breathing became less ragged as he gained control of his emotions.

'My kissing's never reduced a man to tears before,' she joked weakly.

He shook his head. 'Your kissing's great. It's more than great, it's bloody fantastic. You're fantastic.'

'So it's not me it's you?' Fern sighed.

Sam turned to face her, and took her hands in his. 'This time that old cliché really fits,' he said hoarsely.

'It is me. Or rather it's my girlfriend . . . she died. A year ago today.' He closed his eyes in quiet despair and a tear rolled down his cheek, splashing on to the balustrade.

'Oh my God!' Fern's hand rose to cover her mouth. 'I'm so sorry, Sam. That's terrible!'

'You're the first woman I've wanted to kiss since Lucy died,' Sam continued, his voice thick with tears. 'You're gorgeous, Fern, and I really thought I was ready, but I don't think I am. I don't think I ever will be. What am I going to do without her?'

His voice cracked and now he was crying in earnest, big rasping sobs that shook his entire body and spoke of grief so raw that Fern's own eyes filled too. There was nothing she could say, no words of comfort she could offer. All she could do was hold him while he wept, stroking the damp locks of chestnut hair back from his face and letting him cry into her shoulder. Abandoning any hopes of romance Fern listened as he told her about the car crash that had taken his fiancée away from him, soothed him as he explained how guilty he'd felt that he'd not been in the car with her and shushed him as he tried to apologise for ruining her evening. By the time he was all cried out and hailing a taxi home, Fern felt pretty wrung out too and in dire need of a drink.

That M&S dinner for one had never seemed so appealing . . .

Armed with a fresh glass of wine, which it took all of her self-control not to down in one, Fern spotted Pete sitting on a leather sofa and scratching his ears. She smiled. Maybe he was adjusting his mask? They weren't his real ears, after all. Raising a paw he waved at her.

'There you are at last!' Fern said, plopping herself down next to him. 'God, you wouldn't believe the evening I've had! Next time my bloody boss has a good idea about team bonding I'm going to do something more fun, like pull my intestines out through my nose or something!'

The gorilla just nodded. Was he falling asleep? Fern poked him in the ribs. 'Maybe we should both just run away to Prague and work for Alek?'

'Mmm,' said the gorilla.

Scintillating conversation. Not.

Looking around the party for Kim or Jeremy, Fern was suddenly startled to see Pete still on the dance floor, although he was now minus his costume. Her gaze whipped back to King Kong at her side. Wait a minute! If that was Pete who was sitting next to her then? She'd been drinking, but not that heavily! Her eyes couldn't be playing tricks on her after just a few glasses of wine. Fern looked back at the dance floor and sure enough there was the blond good-looking Pete, only now he was busily snogging Clive from IT.

Fern slapped her hand against her forehead and groaned. Fantastic! Cute and single, yes, but nobody had said he was gay. Could this evening get any more embarrassing?

Unfortunately the answer to this question was a resounding yes. Turning to the gorilla Fern grabbed the head and yanked it off, to reveal a very drunken Jeremy who was grinning from ear to ear. Ramming the mask back on, Fern could only hope that he wouldn't remember anything in the morning. In fact, she decided as she knocked back her wine, neither would she! She was going to take a cab home and drink the entire contents of her wine rack.

Collecting her coat and pulling off her wig, she left the party. She really couldn't remember having a worse evening. So much for taking her future into her own hands. Out of all the guys in the place she'd picked one who was an emotional disaster and one who was gay! Maybe she should just become a nun or something? Leave it all to fate after all.

Out in the shadowy street Fern was about to phone for a cab when she heard someone calling her name. Stepping out from the pub opposite into the soft orange streetlight was a muscular figure, smiling widely and clearly overjoyed to see her.

Fern froze. If there was such a thing as fate then surely this was the biggest sign going, a sign that she'd have to be stupid to ignore. Of all the places in the vast sprawling city, and all the times they could both leave parties, they were both right here right now. What were the odds of that happening unless this was her destiny?

The hairs on the back of Fern's neck prickled, because the man crossing the road and striding towards her was none other than Seb.

13

It was the light that woke Fern. Harsh bright slices of sunshine scissored through the blinds and danced across her cheeks before slipping beneath her eyelids. She yawned and burrowed beneath the goose down duvet, enjoying the Egyptian cotton cool and heavy against her skin. With her eyes still shut she stretched her limbs out luxuriously only to encounter a heavy body slumbering beside her.

What!

She wasn't alone.

Cautiously Fern stretched out her arm again and sure enough her fingers encountered warm flesh. Warm, breathing *male* flesh.

Oh. My. God.

What had she done?

Images of the party started to spool through her

memory. There was Jerry grinning drunkenly when she pulled his mask off, Pete kissing Clive from IT and poor grief-stricken Sam weeping on her shoulder. Then the scene shifted and she was outside the party and walking along the street with a familiar muscular frame striding along beside her.

Oh God, not Seb? Surely she wouldn't have? She hadn't drunk that much, surely.

With a mouth drier than the Serengeti she peeled open her eyes. Needles of sunlight stabbed her irises and the dull thud of a headache started to beat in her temples, but for once Fern couldn't give a toss about hangovers. In fact she would gladly mainline Resolve all day or spend hours with her head down the loo in exchange for waking up alone in her own flat. This was just an illusion caused by too much alcohol and dehydration, right? If she shut her eyes and opened them again she'd be curled up in her own small bedroom, listening to Freda's singing or Mrs Latif across the road calling to her children.

But no such luck. When Fern reopened her eyes she wanted to howl. There was no denying it: she was cocooned in an enormous sleigh bed with Seb fast asleep next to her. And what was more she was totally naked.

With a moan Fern snapped her eyes back shut. Just as the daylight was flooding though the ceiling-to-floor windows so images of the night before were illuminating her memory. She saw again the cab drawing up beside them, Seb opening the door to guide her in, before they began to kiss all the way back to Richmond, greedy feverish kisses that left them both hungry for more. She had little recollection of the cab's pulling up outside Seb's apartment but she did recall him scooping her up and carrying her into the bedroom where they'd tumbled on to the bed, pulling off each other's clothes and caressing each other's skin. Fern's cheeks flamed as she recalled how Seb had slid her bra straps from her shoulders and slipped his hands beneath the fabric, his thumbs skimming her nipples and making her moan with need as she hooked her thumbs inside his briefs . . .

Shit! Fern slapped her fist against her forehead. That was the trouble with ex-boyfriends: they knew exactly how to turn you on. And turning Fern on had never been a problem for Seb. It was stopping himself from turning on other girls that had been more of an issue.

She sat up and the world dipped and rolled around her. Swallowing back bile, Fern slid her legs away from Seb's and slowly eased her way from the bed. Seb murmured in his sleep a little before rolling on to his side and starting to snore softly. Fern ran a hand through her tangled curls and looked at him, a mixture of affection and annoyance squeezing her heart. With his skin dark against the white sheets and thick black lashes fanned against his cheeks he looked so perfect in repose that it was almost too easy to forget the pain he'd caused her.

Glancing across the room at the trail of discarded clothes Fern thought ruefully that Seb's kisses must have turned her brain to mush. What had she been thinking? Or maybe the problem was that when Seb made love to her she wasn't capable of thinking at all. He might make her melt, his kisses turning her skin to molten lava, but in the cold light of day he was still the same guy who'd betrayed her with Vanessa. Much as she might want to, how could she ever trust him again?

Now, as she sat on Seb's bed, Fern felt torn. It was wonderful to be back in the flat that still felt like home, bliss to have slept in her old bed; it would be so easy just to pick up where they'd left off. If she woke Seb up now they could make love again before having a long leisurely bath and wandering into Richmond for brunch. Then they could stroll hand in hand through the antique shops, squabbling over which vase or age-spotted mirror to bring home. Her fingers strayed to her kiss-swollen lips. It was such a tempting thought. What if Seb really *was* the one she'd let go?

On the other hand, said a small voice, what if he isn't? What if Vanessa *wasn't* a one-off?

Doubts buzzed through Fern's mind like hornets. If she stayed with Seb those same doubts would sting her day after day until she couldn't bear it any longer. Every time Seb went out she'd be wondering whom he was with; every time he called to say he was running late she'd be tortured by doubts and hideous images of him with other women. Every time he swore that he loved her she'd be wondering how many others had heard the same words and how recently?

Seb had shattered her trust and stolen her peace of mind and without those two precious commodities their relationship was never going to make it.

'Sorry, Seb,' Fern whispered, leaning over and kissing his cheek. 'I'm so sorry.'

Then, without any more hesitation, she gathered up her scattered clothes and slipped from the room. The door clicked shut behind her as Seb slept on.

*

By the time Fern arrived home guilt at running out on Seb had been replaced by relief at being back in her own space. Her flat might be small, it might not have the sweeping views and sharp light of Seb's place, but at least it was hers. It was the refuge where slowly but surely she'd started to rebuild her life apart from Seb, day by day refitting the pieces until one day the gap he'd left had been filled. Fern was over Seb. And the irony was that she'd never realised until this morning.

'I'm never drinking again,' she told Petra as she forked dog food into a bowl. 'I can't believe I actually went home with Seb. What was I thinking?'

But Petra was far too busy eating to pay Fern any attention. 'Sorry for leaving you all alone,' Fern said, scratching the dog between her ears. 'It won't happen again, I promise, and not just because Mum's coming to pick you up either.'

While Petra ate her breakfast Fern took a quick shower, scrubbing herself from head to foot with zesty lime body wash and wishing that she could scrub out the events of the past night just as easily. It wasn't so much that she regretted sleeping with Seb as that she feared she'd given him fresh hope that they'd eventually get back together.

No way is that going to happen. She pulled on jeans and a purple smock top, pushed her feet into her Uggs and squirted herself with scent. Then she pinned her damp curls up on to her head, slicked some lipgloss across her lips and began to feel more human. When Cybil arrived to collect Petra she would never have guessed that her fresh-faced daughter had been out all night.

'Hello, my darling, how are you?' Cybil cried, throwing skinny tanned arms round Petra and smothering the dog with kisses. 'Mummy's missed you so much! Oh yes she has! Has Fern been looking after you, my beautiful baby?'

Fern rolled her eyes. 'Hi, Fern, how are you? Thanks for looking after Petra.'

'Ignore nasty Fern,' Cybil cooed as Petra slobbered doggy kisses all over her. 'She doesn't understand just how much I've missed my baby girl! Oh no she doesn't!'

'Mum! You've only been away a week! She's been fine. I did pop her over to the vet's for a quick check-up, though.'

'My poor baby!' Cybil hugged Petra tightly. 'What was wrong? Why didn't you call me? Is she all right?'

'She's absolutely fine. Honestly, Mum, she's really healthy.'

But Cybil was too busy prising Petra's mouth open and peering down her throat to listen. 'What's wrong? What did the vet say?'

'Mum, will you please stop flapping? She's in perfect health for a dog her age! Matt said there's nothing wrong with her.'

Cybil sat back on her heels and peered at Fern over the top of her Gucci shades. 'Matt? As in lovely vet Matt you dumped to go travelling?'

'Yes.' Fern turned her back on Cybil to fill the kettle and pulled a face. She'd forgotten how taken her mother had been with Matt. In fact the whole Moss family had thought he was Brad Pitt and baby Jesus rolled into one. It'd been a bit wearing after a while.

'Why on earth did you take Petra all the way to Putney to see Matt?' Cybil asked. 'She's got a perfectly good vet in Kingston. Unless ...' she paused, and Fern could practically hear the cogs turning, 'unless you wanted to see Matt?'

Fern slammed the mugs on to the worktop. 'There's nothing wrong with catching up with old friends, Mum. Isn't that what you and what's-his-name have been doing all week?'

Cybil ignored the dig. 'I don't blame you if you have regrets about Matt, darling. Tamsin was only saying the other day what a great opportunity you missed there. You should've married Matt when you had the chance. He had his life so well sorted. You would've been really comfortable and secure with him.'

'And that's a reason to marry someone, is it?' Fern rounded on her mother. 'Being secure is all that counts?'

'There's a lot to be said for security, darling. And dear Matt was always so kind to animals.'

'Well excuse me if I want a bit more than a man who puts animal welfare before my needs!'

Cybil looked hurt. 'That wasn't what I meant. I just thought that after Daddy . . .' Her voice tailed off. 'I meant it must be nice to be taken care of.'

Fern flushed. She hadn't meant to criticise her mother. Cybil had always done her best. It wasn't really her fault that her parenting skills were better suited to dogs than to children.

'Mum, I know you mean well but I really, really don't want to talk about Matt.'

'Well, maybe not,' Cybil sighed. 'But darling, please don't look at me as some kind of relationship role model. Besides, Tamsin had a point. Matt is wonderful husband material.'

'Then Tamsin should have married him if she

thinks he's so great!' Fern snapped, missing the coffee cups in her annoyance and sloshing hot water all over the worktop. 'It's too late now, anyway. Matt's engaged to another vet called Amanda who likes animals and mud every bit as much as he does. He really isn't interested in me.' *Or he would have called*, she added silently.

Seeing the strength of her daughter's feeling – and eyeing the kettle nervously – Cybil changed the subject.

'And how are you, darling? Is work going well?'

'It's fine.' Fern carried the heavy ceramic mugs to the table and sat down opposite her mother. 'I'm working on *Cymbeline* at the moment.'

Cybil sighed. 'A wonderful play. Did I tell you I once played Imogen at the Swan? Such a sad play, so much loss and despair.'

Fern chewed her thumbnail. Loss and despair just about summed up her life lately. The same thought had obviously occurred to Cybil, who said gently, 'I'm sorry, Fern. That was tactless of me. I know you're still upset about breaking up with Seb.'

'It's partly that,' said Fern, chewing off another bit of nail. God, if she started thinking about Seb she'd be nailless by lunchtime. He was bound to have woken up by now and discovered that she'd done a runner. Was he angry? Or was he upset? She wasn't sure which scenario was worse. She only hoped he wasn't about to turn up on the doorstep and suffocate her with alliums.

'Only partly? So what else is worrying you?' Cybil reached across the table and covered Fern's hand with her own, so deeply tanned it looked as though she'd dipped it in treacle. 'You can tell me, you know.'

Touched by Cybil's concern Fern found herself pouring out the story of Zoe's hen night and the scarily accurate reading that Angela had given her. Cybil listened without interrupting, only paling a little beneath her tan when Fern told her how the psychic had known all about Roger's death.

'So,' Fern said finally, 'I guess it's all started to get to me. I can't help thinking about all the guys I used to date and wondering whether I should have made it work with one of them. That's why I went to see Matt. I needed to find out if he was the one I let go.'

And that's also why I stayed the night with Seb, she added silently. I may have been drunk, but deep down I wanted to see if I could forget about Vanessa and build a future with him.

Cybil frowned. 'For what it's worth I think you should ignore it all, darling. Prophecies ought to be about the future, not the past. It's time you moved forward and got on with your life rather than dwelling on what could have been.' She shuddered theatrically. 'There's something rather morbid about chasing after ghosts.'

Fern was surprised. She'd expected Cybil to be all for dramatics and tracking down lost soulmates. 'Do you really think its nonsense?'

'Of course!' Cybil said firmly. 'She just managed to string some lucky guesses together, that's all. You're a beautiful girl with your whole life ahead of you. There's absolutely nothing to worry about. When the right man comes along you won't need a psychic to help you find him.'

'You're right,' said Fern with relief. 'I'll just look forward from now on.'

After that their conversation turned back to Petra and Tamsin's new retriever puppy, which was much safer ground. By the time her mother departed in a cloud of exotic perfume Fern was feeling far more cheerful. Things were clear with Matt, she knew in her heart that she was over Seb, and she was ready to move on.

As she tidied the kitchen Fern pressed play on her answerphone, smiling when Jeremy apologised for being so drunk that he hadn't escorted her and

Kim home and smiling even more widely at Kim's breathless message extolling the virtues of Charlie Chaplin. The third message turned her smile into a grin. It was Alek. She'd know that sexy European accent and deep velvety timbre anywhere.

'Why are all the good ones taken?' Fern sighed. It was one of life's eternal mysteries, like where do flies go in the winter or why does the sale bargain outfit never look good when you get it home?

'Hey, Fern,' Alek was saying. 'When you get this message call me, yes? It's been a while since we had a good chat. In fact, Francesca and I were just saying that you ought to come out for a long weekend. I'm pretty busy working on the new Luke Scottman movie but I'd be more than happy to take a break and show you the sights. Anyway, hope you're okay. Talk soon!'

All the breath left Fern's body as though a hippo had landed on her chest.

Alek was working with Luke? This had to be a sign! It couldn't just be coincidence. Fate was telling her that she had to fly to Prague and see Luke again.

Before she had time to change her mind, or remind herself of her new resolve to forget all about the hen night prophecy, Fern's fingers were flying over the key pad to call Alek back and take him up on his offer of a weekend in Prague. After the trauma with Matt she certainly deserved a holiday and some space away from Seb might come in handy too.

And as for Luke Scottman . . . well, that was one ghost she really would love to see in the well-toned flesh!

14

The moon was riding high above Prague like a smile in the night-time sky, silvering the Vltava river and trickling ribbons of light across the ancient spires and rooftops. Fern leaned her hands on the wall of the roof garden and sighed with pleasure. The city was everything that Alek had promised and she could hardly believe her luck in being here. She was glad Jeremy had given her a week's holiday at such short notice. She'd need way more than a long weekend to fit in all the sightseeing.

'Do you like it?' Alek said over her shoulder as he too gazed at the twinkling lights of the slumbering city. His house was just off Wenceslas Square, and from the roof terrace the ancient bridges and cobbled streets were so close that Fern could almost reach out and touch them.

'Like it?' she breathed. 'It's absolutely magical! I

totally understand now why you were so keen to move here.'

Alek laughed. 'I hate to say I told you so! But seriously, aren't you tempted to move out here and work with me? Apart from the fact that you obviously miss me like crazy, the city is fantastic!'

Fern sighed. Tempted didn't even come close. Prague was beautiful, Alek and Francesca were warm and welcoming and best of all she was miles away from Matt and Seb and the whole prophecy mess. The thought of starting a new life in this stunning city had never been more appealing.

'I'm very tempted,' she admitted, 'especially when I see beautiful houses like this one. It certainly puts my place in the shade.'

Alek and Francesca lived in an elegant eighteenth-century townhouse that was brimming with character. The outside was covered in ornate cornicing like a dream wedding cake and the inside was all cool flagstone hallways and polished oak floors. Although the house was tall and narrow Alek's innate sense of style made it feel light and spacious with just the right marriage of modernity and classic style. Fern loved it, especially this surprising oasis of a roof garden with its pots of fragrant rosemary and lavender and tumbling flowers.

Tooting just couldn't compete.

'Come and work with me and you could buy one just like it,' Alek promised her. 'You know you want to! Think of the fun we could have. And did I mention that I have been asked to tender for the set design on the new Bond movie?'

'Only about a million times a minute since I got here!' Fern grinned. 'But even Daniel Craig can't tempt me, I'm afraid, Al. I'm still very happy working with Jeremy. Besides, like I said before, my friends and family are all in England. I'd really miss them if I moved abroad.'

'You can fly home in two hours,' Alek pointed out. 'And you will make many new friends here. Just look at how everyone loved you tonight! In fact, they've sent me to fetch you back down.' He raised a dark eyebrow. 'I think several of the guys have their eye on you, Ms Moss!'

She swatted him on the arm. 'They're just being kind. Everyone's so friendly.'

'But of course! I've been singing your praises ever since I moved here. Everyone's been dying to meet you. I couldn't have kept them away if I tried!'

To celebrate Fern's first evening in Prague Alek and Francesca had invited a small group of friends over for dinner. Alek adored cooking, his creativity spilling into his culinary expertise, and tonight's five-course meal had been a delight. The wine and conversation had flowed and the atmosphere was so relaxed that Fern had found herself chatting to total strangers with ease.

'Your friends are great,' she told him. 'They've made me feel so welcome.'

Alek squeezed her shoulder as he followed her down the spiral staircase and back into the kitchen. 'That's because you *are* welcome. And Tomas, I think, is particularly taken! I shall have to give him a serious talking to about protecting your honour.'

'I'm perfectly safe, Al. He's just being friendly.' Fern laughed. Tomas the tour guide, with his mane of tousled dirty-blond hair and merry, faded khaki eyes, was certainly attractive but way out of her league. He looked like a carving by Michelangelo using Brad Pitt as a model. 'Anyway, he's only touting for business. He's already offered to give me a private tour of the city.'

'I bet he has,' said Alek darkly. 'When he offers to show you his etchings run fast, okay? Tomas has quite a reputation.'

'Thanks for the warning but there's no way I'd get involved with Tomas. After Seb I think I'm off men for good.'

Alek scowled. He'd disliked Seb practically from the moment that Fern had introduced them. She'd been surprised, because Alek usually had a disposition sunnier than the Caribbean and his black mood had been totally out of character. Seb had made sarky comments about Alek's being jealous but Fern had known that was rubbish. She and Alek had only ever been good friends. He was usually joined at the hip to some glamorous leggy model type who was about as much like Fern as chalk was to cheese. Being small and quirky Fern knew she wasn't Alek's type so she just had to accept that for some inexplicable reason he disliked Seb. Fortunately Alek had hooked up with Chess a few weeks later and the situation had calmed down. Cosy dinners for four had never been on the agenda, though, and on the rare occasion that the couples did meet up the atmosphere between the two guys had made the ice age look tropical.

'Once a cheat always a cheat, Fern. You deserve so much better,' was all Alek said now, turning his attention to the coffee machine and grinding the beans with a grim expression. If they were voodoo beans, thought Fern, Seb would be clutching his balls and yelping right now. Thoughtfully she twisted a curl round her finger. 'I know it's stupid, but I can't help wondering if maybe it was my fault that he went off with Vanessa. I was working long hours and I suppose he was feeling neglected.'

Alek spun round to face her, his eyes glittering with anger.

'You're right, it is stupid! In fact that's the biggest load of nonsense I think I have ever heard! He's an adult, Fern, not some pathetic lonely teenager. Of course you work long hours. We all do, it's called having a career. Why is it that some people find that so hard to understand? If Seb couldn't handle that then he's the inadequate one, not you, and he's an even bigger dickhead than I think he is already for losing you.'

Something bleak shadowed Alek's face for a second. Fern was taken aback. Was this outburst just about her, or was there more to it? She held up her hands. 'I wasn't making excuses for Seb; I was just trying to understand things from his perspective. Set design does put pressure on a relationship.'

Alek shrugged. 'Maybe so, but if you love someone you support them in their career, yes? You don't use it as an excuse to cheat on them.' His scowl seemed to deepen and Fern could have kicked herself for raising the subject. Alek's artistic temperament was given to extremes of emotion.

Like the leaving party she'd thrown for him, for instance. He'd been almost unable to speak when they'd said goodbye. Alek, unlike bloody Seb, felt things deeply. He was honest and loyal and true, which probably made him the antithesis of Seb, who might just about recognise these qualities if they did a naked tap dance in front of him.

'You're right. Let's forget about Seb. I've wasted far too much energy on him for one lifetime.' She smiled brightly. 'Now, Mr Novak, how about putting some alcohol in those coffees?'

'You still like a shot of Tia Maria in yours, yes?'

'Guilty as charged. You have a good memory, Alek.'

'Of course I remember. I'll never forget any of the things we did and the times we shared. They were some of the best of my life. Do you remember the night we drove down to Brighton and watched the sun come up? Or the time we all hired that canal barge?'

'What about the time you decided to take me and Jeremy rowing and dropped an oar?' Fern recalled. 'I'll never forget that!'

'Yes, okay!' Waving his hands as though to swat away the memory, Alek pretended to be absorbed by his complex coffee machine before groaning, 'Now

I'm really embarrassed! Why did you have to bring up that particular episode?'

'Because it was so funny! Especially when you jumped in and swam after the oar. You were picking pond weed out of your hair for hours!'

'That's why I've cut it,' Alek deadpanned. 'In case I ever get the urge to take you rowing on the Vltava.' He'd cropped his hair since Fern had last seen him and now it was moleskin short. It suited him, she found herself thinking; it accentuated his sharp cheekbones and pitch dark eyes.

'I thought the pond slime look really suited you,' she giggled.

'That's it. I can't take any more of this humiliation!' Alek said, placing his hand in the small of Fern's back and giving her a push. 'Leave me to make the coffee and restore my wounded pride in peace!'

Laughing, Fern wandered back into the sitting room and was soon deep in conversation with Eliska, who worked on the editorial staff of a women's magazine, and Tomas, who crossed the room to join them. Eliska described some of her favourite places in the city and insisted that Fern visit them, while Tomas nodded frantically like the dog in the Churchill advert.

'Prague can be a complicated place to get about

if you are a visitor,' he said, his moss-green eyes serious as he went on to describe the system of ten *prahas*, or districts, that the city was divided into. 'I'll show you the Loreta and the Dancing House, and of course the Josefov – the Spanish synagogue is very beautiful and not to be missed.'

'That's really kind, but I'm not here for long and I'm sure Alek will show me round,' said Fern quickly. The last thing she wanted was to commit herself to anything that could get in the way of meeting Luke or give Tomas the wrong idea.

'I'd take Tomas up on his offer if I were you,' interrupted Francesca. 'All Alek does these days is work. He hardly has time for any of us.'

Fern looked up in surprise and noticed for the first time the blue smudges beneath Francesca's eyes and the rigid set of her mouth. Francesca worked in a merchant bank and over dinner had been complaining that the economic downturn was making life very difficult, but her sharp comment was unexpected and very out of character.

'Alek's always been passionate about his work,' Fern said gently, not liking to hear anyone say anything negative about her friend. 'And set design doesn't have regular hours.'

'Don't I know it,' Francesca said bitterly. 'Alek

never stops telling me that, on the rare occasions that I do see him.'

Tomas and Eliska looked away, embarrassed. Fern frowned. 'Alek loves his work, Chess. He always has done, but he loves you too.'

Francesca looked as though she was about to say something in response, but then she gathered herself visibly and gave Fern a tight smile.

'Ignore me – I'm just being grumpy. Sorry, guys. I didn't mean to snap, but I'm very tired. Some of us have to be up early in the morning and I've been on the go since four thirty. The markets don't care if I've been awake half the night.'

'You poor bankers have to get up much earlier than we creative types,' Eliska said sympathetically.

'Indeed we do.' Francesca rose to her feet and smothered a yawn. 'So I'm going to call it a day and go to bed. Night, everyone.'

She left the room to a chorus of goodnights but something about the stiffness of her mouth and the rigid set of her shoulders made Fern uneasy. There was an undercurrent of tension between Chess and Alek that she hadn't noticed before. Although they'd both gone out of their way to make her feel at home she hoped that her presence in the house wasn't putting a strain on them.

'There, even Chess says that Alek's busy!' Pressing his advantage, Tomas handed Fern his card. 'You can't miss the chance to explore the most beautiful city in the world. I'm only too happy to show you round while he has to work.'

Fern gave in and took it. 'Thanks. That's really kind of you.'

'It will be my pleasure. Why don't you pop my number into your mobile?'

She laughed. 'You don't give up easily!'

'I certainly don't when a beautiful woman is involved,' said Tomas, giving her a slow, sexy smile. Fern laughed again. Wow. Maybe she should move to Prague if this was the response she got. She couldn't help finding his cheesy chat-up lines funny, though.

'You win!' She picked her mobile up from the coffee table and started to punch his number in. 'I'll call you tomorrow.'

'I'll look forward to it,' said Tomas.

'That didn't take long,' remarked Alek, entering the room with a tray of coffee and a selection of liqueurs and glancing across at Fern as she fiddled with her mobile. He didn't look particularly impressed but she chose to ignore him. Alek meant well but she was a big girl. Hitting Prague with

Tomas could be a lot of fun, and after all she was on holiday.

Tomas grinned. 'Some of us have it, Alek, some of us don't. Even Chess has given up with you tonight.'

Alek set the tray down. 'Where's she gone? Is she okay?'

'She went to bed,' said Fern. 'She seems a bit stressed.'

Alek said nothing but sloshed a generous measure of Tia Maria into Fern's cup and then did the same for his own. It was going to be one of those evenings then, she thought, when they'd get so drunk they wouldn't even notice if the coffee cups started dancing the cancan.

'Chess is looking very tired. Your lovely girlfriend works too hard, Alek,' said Eliska, leaning forward to accept an espresso. Fern couldn't help admiring her elegance. From the flawless manicure to the timeless Chanel suit and Christian Louboutins everything about her spoke of sophistication. Maybe Fern should squeeze in a spot of shopping while she was here. Or were some women just born effortlessly groomed?

Alek's brows drew together in a concerned expression. 'You know Chess, Eliska. She loves the regimented world of banking even if it half kills her.

If you'll excuse me for a minute I'll just go and check that she's all right.'

Alek left them but the conversation continued to ebb and flow like the tide. Fern sank into the leather sofa and listened as Tomas described the St Charles Bridge and the magnificence of the cathedral. She nodded and sipped her coffee, the warmth and the alcohol uncurling pleasantly in her stomach, and was just thinking how relaxed she felt when the discordant sound of raised voices scraped the atmosphere. Eliska caught her eye and raised her shoulders quizzically. Moments later the voices were replaced by the thud of Alek's footfalls on the stair treads. When he entered the sitting room his cheeks were flushed and his eyes were glittering.

An icy hand clenched round Fern's heart. She'd never seen so much as a hint of discord between Alek and Francesca before. What was going on?

'Chess has got an early start tomorrow,' he said tightly, helping himself to coffee and sitting down. 'So it looks like it's just us arty types pushing on till dawn.'

'Now I have you to myself at last,' Eliska said to Fern as he engaged Tomas in a discussion about politics, 'I was wondering if you would consider doing an interview for my magazine?'

Fern nearly choked on her coffee. 'Really? Are you serious? Why would you want to do that?' The difference between the elegant Czech woman in couture and Fern in her orange and pink maxi dress from Miss Selfridge couldn't have been more apparent, and Fern was pretty sure that Eliska's readers wouldn't aspire to bitten nails and glittery hair slides from Accessorize.

But Eliska was serious. 'Our readers would adore hearing about your life in London. Maybe we could combine it with a trip to one of Prague's theatres? I know Alek's recently finished work at the Laterna Magika. It would be great fun for you to see his work again.'

Fern felt a thrill of excitement. 'I'd love that. Thank you!'

Eliska shook her blond head. 'No, Fern, thank you. I think it'll be a lot of fun.'

'Don't monopolise her too much,' interrupted Alek sternly. 'Tomas has already told me that he's claimed Fern for a day touring the city. She's supposed to be on holiday!'

'I'm enjoying being so popular,' said Fern. 'I should have come to Prague before.'

'Yes,' said Alek softly, his gaze catching Fern's. 'You should.'

*

By the time the last guest had kissed her goodbye and slipped out into the velvety darkness, Fern felt sleepy with good food and her eyes were lead heavy. Already she was looking forward to climbing the stairs to the pretty guest bedroom and burrowing under the heavy duvet. But Alek, it seemed, had other ideas and poured them both a large brandy.

'God, Alek,' Fern exclaimed, swirling the amber liquid in the bell glass. 'I'll never climb the stairs if I drink all this!'

'Good, then at least I'll have you to myself for a bit. Tomas totally monopolised you all night,' he teased.

Fern blushed and tried to hide her pink cheeks by pretending to be fascinated by the cognac. 'He's very sweet.'

'Just sweet? He'd be devastated to hear you say that!' Alek raised her chin with his forefinger. 'You're blushing! Do I take that to mean that you like our friendly tour guide?'

'Stop it!' Fern giggled. 'He's a nice guy but I don't like him in *that* way.'

'You can't let Seb put you off men for ever. We're not all cheating bastards, you know. I know Tomas is a bit of a ladies' man but maybe I was a bit harsh earlier. He's not a bad guy. If you were to go for a drink or something, maybe Chess and I could come too?'

'I'm not interested in dating Tomas,' Fern told Alek firmly. 'Or anyone.'

'Fern, you're gorgeous, and sexy and fun,' said Alek.

Blimey, thought Fern, he *has* been drinking! She laughed. 'Thanks! It's good to know my friends still love me!'

'Everyone loves you. There are lots of guys who'd love to date you. If I was single I'd be right in the front of the queue,' said Alek gallantly.

'I don't see a queue, but thanks anyway.' She paused and took a sip of her drink. Comforting fiery warmth uncoiled through her limbs and ignited her courage. *Sod it, I'm going to tell him.* Alek was one of her dearest friends; he'd understand why she needed to find Luke. He'd be sympathetic and supportive, unlike her mother.

'I'm kind of here because of someone,' she said slowly. 'I haven't told him yet but I'm hoping he'll feel the same way.'

Alek's pupils were inky dark. When he spoke his voice was hoarse. 'Who is it?'

Fern took a deep breath. 'It's Luke Scottman;

remember that I dated him at uni?' Leaving out the bit about Angela's predictions – Alek might be lovely but he was still a bloke and therefore hardwired to scoff at psychic stuff – she confessed she had a feeling that there was unfinished business between herself and Luke, and however outrageous it may sound she really needed to see him so she could put her mind at rest. While she spoke Alek remained silent, his head tilted slightly and his white teeth biting his full bottom lip as he contemplated what she was saying. Not once did he interrupt or judge her. In fact he could have been carved from granite except for a muscle that leapt in his cheek.

'I've just got this hideous fear that I may have let someone special get away from me,' Fern sighed. 'And I know for sure it isn't Seb. Maybe Luke and I shouldn't have broken up. I know he didn't really want to at the time but I was so scared about the uncertainty of being with an actor.' She stared miserably into her glass. 'Oh, Al. What if I got it all wrong and he was the love of my life after all?'

Alek sighed heavily and refilled his glass. 'Relationships are uncertain, Fern. They don't come with guarantees.'

Fern knew he was thinking about his argument with Francesca. 'Are you and Chess okay, Alek?'

'I don't know,' he said quietly. 'You know Chess. She likes everything ordered and neat but set design just doesn't work like that, especially on a film location. I can't always guarantee when I'll be at home and when I call to break arrangements she goes crazy.'

Fern understood totally. A set designer's hours were never nine to five. The wrong light, an actor's tantrum, the wrong shade of paint; any of those could stretch two hours into six.

'It can be really hard on partners,' she agreed. 'Seb used to hate it that I was always having to change our plans or work late.'

'Maybe you have to be in it to actually understand. Things are always really good between us when I'm in between movies or at the planning stages of a project, because then I work a tight schedule, but as soon as I'm working on set my time's not my own and she hates it. That's what this evening was really about. I'd told her I'd be on location for most of next week and she isn't happy. What can I do, though?'

Fern didn't have a clue. If she did maybe she wouldn't still be single.

'She's started hinting that she wants to relocate to the countryside,' Alek continued. 'I know she wants to move us to the next level: marriage, children . . .

the full works . . .' His voice tailed off and he took another slug of his brandy.

Fern sighed. 'I suppose it's only natural when you reach your thirties.'

Alek shrugged. 'Maybe, but I just don't feel ready for that yet. I really enjoy living in the city and I love my work. It's a whirlwind life but I love not knowing what's coming from one day to the next. I can't imagine always working in the same place and doing the same things, can you?'

She shook her head. 'I know exactly what you mean. But can you ever hope to find someone who wants the same things you do?'

'It certainly puts a strain on a relationship when you don't,' he said sadly. 'God, listen to me whinging! Sorry, Fern – this isn't a very cheerful start to your holiday. Ignore me. I'm sure Chess and I will sort it out.'

Fern squeezed his hand. 'I hope so, Alek, I really do. You're such a great couple. My being here isn't making things difficult, is it?'

'No! Of course not! God! Chess would kill me if she knew you thought that!' Alek gave Fern a bright smile which didn't quite reach his eyes. 'Anyway, enough of me. We need to think of a way for you to meet Luke.'

'Is it going to be difficult then?' Fern hadn't expected that. Maybe she was naive, but she'd thought she'd pop over to the set of Luke's film and say hello, then they'd go for lunch and talk about old times.

'Nice idea,' said Alek when Fern revealed this master plan, 'but there's one massive flaw: Luke's a major film star now and he's got the security that goes with the territory. Fans are always trying to get to him. Besides, the shoot is two weeks behind schedule and we're desperately busy. I did invite Luke over to join us this evening because you're here but I wasn't surprised when he sent his apologies.'

Fern's heart plopped into her pink wedge heels. She'd been so sure Luke would be as keen to meet as she was and that he'd turn out to be her soulmate that she hadn't considered a back-up plan.

'Don't worry,' said Alek, seeing her face fall, 'I won't give up. Filming's going to be intense but I'm sure I'll catch up with Luke eventually. Come to work with me tomorrow. Maybe you'll bump into him yourself.'

Fern yawned widely. 'Mmm. Okay.'

Alek took her empty glass. 'Go on, up to bed and get some beauty sleep just in case you bump into the elusive Mr Scottman tomorrow. You're competing with supermodels now, you know!'

Fern didn't need telling twice. She was so tired that it was almost too much effort to haul herself out of the chair and make her weary way up to her bedroom. As she climbed the stairs her heart felt as heavy as her eyes. Would she get to see Luke tomorrow? And would he even want to see her? After all, he'd come a long way since they'd been poor students together. She'd read enough tabloids to know that Luke had dated some of the most beautiful women in the world. Why on earth would he be interested in her?

Her mother was right. It really was time she stopped going off at things half cocked. Alek's phone message had seemed to promise the perfect solution to finding out whether or not Luke was the one she'd let go; now Fern wasn't quite so sure.

In fact she wasn't sure at all.

15

Twilight seeped across Prague as the daylight leached from the sky, the golds and pinks of sunset succumbing to purples and dusky indigos as long shadows began to pool across the worn cobbles. The sun was just a crimson fingernail above the rooftops, its dying rays blushing the ancient stone buildings, while the River Vltava wound its way slowly through the city, carrying the swans along as effortlessly as passengers on an airport walkway.

This had to be the most romantic city in the world, thought Fern wistfully as she stood by the Lesser Tower and surveyed the view. No wonder the location scouts had chosen it for *Dynamite*. The St Charles Bridge was everything that Tomas had promised; the towers were like something out of a fairy tale, and she felt really glad she'd decided to explore a little before she met Alek and Francesca for dinner. It didn't matter that the far end of the bridge was closed for the film crew; from her vantage point Fern could see more than enough. The avenue of statues that stretched right across the bridge took her breath away and in the fading light their worn faces seemed to shift and follow her footsteps with unseeing eyes.

A light mist hugged the river bank and Fern shivered. The day had been unseasonably warm and when she'd woken up from a blissfully heavy sleep a gold medallion sun had beamed down from a cloudless sky. She'd changed her mind about going to work with Alek, and instead had spent a happy hour having lunch at a pavement café and studying her Rough Guide before exploring the city. But now that the sun had slipped below the rooftops she was starting to feel a bit chilly in her floaty dress and sandals. Maybe it was time she went back to Alek's and changed before dinner? She could always see the bridge another day; after all, Tomas was only a call away.

Just as she was about to turn for home Fern's eye was caught by a man standing at the far side of the bridge. Broad-shouldered and wearing a tux with the tie loosened he was the sort of man who made you look twice and then come back for a third glance. His thick honey-blond hair lifted in the evening breeze and even from her distant vantage point Fern could see the wall-to-wall grin that split his face and made his eyes crinkle as he waved at her from across a bank of film cameras. Fern felt her breath catch in her throat as her heart started to play squash against her ribcage. It couldn't be . . .

Could it?

Striding across the bridge towards her was none other than Luke Scottman.

'Fern! It really is you!' Before she even had the chance to collect her thoughts he swung her up into his arms and twirled her round. 'I'd know those blond curls anywhere! I can't believe it's you!'

'Of course it's me,' Fern said, hugging him back and thinking how good it felt to be held by him. 'I'm so glad to see you, Luke! This is such a lovely surprise!'

Nodding his agreement Luke kept her clasped against his muscular body until Fern thought she'd pass out with the myriad sensations rippling through her. His lips grazed her temples and suddenly she was eighteen again and so passionately in love that it hurt. He even still smelt like the old Luke: something spicy and so deliciously male that she shivered.

'It's good to see you too,' Luke whispered into

her hair. 'When I heard you were in town I really hoped we'd catch up. I couldn't believe it when I saw you standing on the bridge.' He smiled ruefully. 'I think I've just wrecked a take by dashing away to see you.'

He lowered her to the ground, sliding her slowly down the length of his strong body, but his hands remained on her shoulder blades, his fingers gently tracing her collarbones. Suddenly Fern was tongue-tied. He still looked like her Luke but he had the gloss and confidence of the very successful and wealthy. It was also really weird to see someone in the flesh that she was more used to seeing in *OK!* magazine.

'You look really well,' was all she managed to say and then could have ripped her tongue out. Here she was in the arms of one of the sexiest men in film, and possibly the love of her life to boot, and all she could come out with was a lame comment like that?

But Luke didn't seem bothered. 'And you look sensational! That dress is amazing, especially when the light shines right through it. You always did have the sexiest legs!'

Fern felt her cheeks turn so pink that if she stood on one leg she'd pass for a flamingo. Luke's grin was wider than a jack-o'-lantern's, and she was nearly blinded by the whiteness of his teeth. That was enough to bring her to her senses. This wasn't her big comfort blanket university boyfriend any more; this groomed and well-honed man was Luke Scottman the A-list movie star and the fantasy figure of most red-blooded women. She mustn't make the same mistake she'd made with Matt and assume that nothing had changed in the time they'd been apart. They were both very different people now.

She peered over his shoulder. 'Er, Luke, there're lots of people running after you.'

He grimaced. 'Bloody hell! That'll be my PR team. They monitor my every move and I'm not allowed to do anything they don't approve of.' He stepped back, breaking their embrace. 'They've come to drag me back to work.'

'Really?' Already Fern could feel the heat of resentment from the pretty clipboard-carrying girls swarming towards him like frantic wasps. 'That doesn't sound like much fun. What's the point of being a big movie star if you can't relax when you feel the need? Whatever happened to all the hedonism and hot tubs?'

Luke ran a hand through his rumpled blond hair.

'There's no time for that! Besides, it's all wheatgrass juice, pumping iron and organic vegetables now. I can't remember the last time I had fun.' His big, generous mouth curled into a smile. 'We used to have a lot of it, though, didn't we?'

That sexy smile transported Fern back twelve years faster than you could say time machine. For a second she was back in the university halls of residence and curled up with Luke in a narrow bed, her sides aching with laughter as they experimented with a tub of chocolate body paint before tumbling out on to the floor . . .

'They're good memories, aren't they?' he murmured. 'I always loved the way you blush so easily. Listen, Fern, we really need to—'

But what they needed to do Fern didn't discover because the whirlwind of PR girls had caught up and surrounded Luke, braying at him about schedules and the state of the light. Luke rolled his eyes.

'Looks like I'd better get back. No rest for the wicked.'

'No wonder you're busy then!' Fern teased. 'I'll leave you to it.'

'Fern, wait,' Luke said as he was attacked by one girl wielding a powder puff and another with the most enormous can of hairspray. 'We can't talk now but I must see you again, if that's okay?'

His blue eyes clouded with uncertainty and Fern's heart melted. She'd never been able to resist Luke. 'Of course it's okay,' she said.

Luke snapped his fingers at the horsey-looking blonde who was glaring at Fern, her mouth like a paper cut. 'Emily, I want you to take this lady's mobile number for me.'

'Yes, Mr Scottman,' simpered Emily, suddenly all smiles and flourishing a pen and notebook. The look she shot at Fern should have laid her out on the floor and said *What the hell does he want your number for?* It was a good point. Fern wasn't exactly certain herself.

'Mr Scottman, the director's frantic,' piped up another member of the PR coven. 'He says you need to be back on the set immediately.'

Luke pulled a face. 'See what I'm up against?' Then he was whisked away back to the set, mouthing *I'll call you* over glossy blond heads, leaving Fern alone again on the bridge. But as he turned for a last time and blew an exaggerated kiss, her heart rose like a hot air balloon. Bumping into Luke like this had to be fate. What other explanation could there be? He had to be the one she'd let go!

*

Two days later Fern's hot air balloon had well and truly popped. Luke had texted once to say he'd still love to see her but unfortunately hadn't got a window in the hectic shooting schedule. Since then her phone had remained stubbornly silent.

'Stop checking that bloody phone!' Alek scolded Fern when she gazed at the screen for the umpteenth time. 'There's absolutely no correlation between you looking at it and Luke Scottman deciding to call.'

'Sorry, Alek.' Fern knew she was being ridiculous but she seemed to have the text-checking equivalent of Tourette's. 'I'm turning it off now.'

'Thank God,' said Alek. 'Now all we need is for the rain to stop and the day may actually start to look up.'

Fern was on set with Alek in a pretty medieval square which had been roped off for shooting (no sign of Luke because these scenes involved his co-star) and the heavens had well and truly opened. Despite huddling beneath Alek's large umbrella her combats were soaked right through to her knickers and raindrops were trickling down her neck. They passed the time by drinking strong coffee brewed by the catering crew and discussing the exciting plans that Alek had for his company. Fern was so carried away by his enthusiasm that she stopped noticing the rain and it came as a surprise when Alek pointed out that the skies were clearing.

She could chat to Alek all day long and never run out of things to say, Fern thought as she helped him remove tarpaulins from a café set. He was such good company and it made a pleasant change to spend time with someone who totally surfed on her wavelength rather than telling her off for her butterfly mind. Alek's thoughts also ran around like mercury but somehow they managed to work together in perfect harmony. Straightening a tablecloth, Fern felt a pang of sadness. They made such a good team, and helping Alex out on set only reminded her how much she missed working with him.

'Oh, for God's sake,' Alek exclaimed, pointing across the square. 'What is it about a roped-off area that these idiots don't understand?'

A group of English lads – she could tell they were English from their baggy Man U strip and pallid, unhealthy faces. No self-respecting Czech would be seen dead looking like that – had clambered over the ropes and were lumbering towards the café set. Plonking themselves down at a table they began a loud and drunken discussion about getting their stag night on the television. In spite of her annoyance Fern couldn't help smiling. It was as if the cast of *Shameless* had wandered on to the set of a Bond movie.

With a face like thunder Alek threw his tarpaulin down and strode towards the interlopers.

'Can you move on, please? This is a film set and you're holding up a shoot.'

As usual when Alek got upset his accent became more pronounced and the lads looked puzzled. One of them peered up from underneath his baseball cap.

'What's that, mate? I don't speak Pragueish.'

'I said you need to move!' snapped Alek. 'We're shooting a film here.'

Baseball Cap, who was clearly the leader, stuck his chin out belligerently. 'Not until we've had a beer!'

Alek threw his hands in the air in exasperation. 'I don't have time for this. I'll call security and have you thrown out if that's what it takes.'

Baseball Cap jumped to his feet. Although flabby he was six feet tall and judging by his broken nose no stranger to fights. Alek at five ten was lithe and toned but no match for eighteen stone of drunken stupidity. The last thing Fern wanted was to see him get beaten up.

'Hey guys, if I can fix you a free beer will you move on?' Fern said quickly as an idea started to take shape. 'We really don't want any trouble. We just need to shoot this scene.'

There was a chorus of yeahs at this suggestion and instantly the mood lightened. Now all she had to do was find the free beer. Switching on her mobile she scrolled through the contacts to Tomas, who was delighted to hear from her. Minutes later she'd managed to get the directions to a nearby bar and a promise from Tomas to fix it with the owners to give the English boys a free Stella each. Ringing off with a promise to meet him the next day Fern felt very glad she'd taken his number, although she was starting to wonder about how he'd expect her to repay him.

She'd worry about that tomorrow. At the moment she had enough on her plate trying to move on six drunken lads.

'Right,' she said, snapping the phone shut, 'there's free beer for all of you at Zlata's Bar. It's just off the square and down Nicolas Street.'

Mollified, the lads moved on, cheering and calling for Fern to join them, but she declined, laughing. 'Some of us have got work to do!'

Alek stood and watched the scene with his arms folded and an admiring look on his face.

'Come with us and leave that miserable bastard behind,' hollered Baseball Cap. 'We'll show you a better time than he could!'

Ignoring him Fern called back, 'It's left out of the square and then third street on the right. Zlata's Bar. Enjoy!' and with much singing and cheering the lads ambled away.

'You are amazing, do you know that?' Alek said with a smile. After his anger it was like the sun coming out from behind a cloud. He had a lovely smile, Fern thought. It might not be cosmetically perfect like Luke's was these days but there was something irresistibly warm about it.

'I aim to please!'

'You certainly manage that. I really appreciated what you just did there. I thought I was going to lose it.' Alek shook his head. 'Are you sure you won't come and work with me? We make such a great team.'

Fern bit her lip. She could hardly tell him she was waiting on a psychic's prophecy before she moved on with her life; he'd think she'd lost the plot. Maybe in some small way she had.

Sensing her indecision Alek added, 'I'd make you a partner, Fern. It'd be worth it, I promise. No one would be able to compete with us. It'd be amazing!'

She sighed. 'I wish I could but this really isn't the right time for me to move away, Alek. Maybe in the future?'

'You can't blame a guy for trying,' he sighed, looking disappointed, 'but the offer's there if you change your mind.'

'Thanks, I do appreciate it. It's just that things are a bit complicated right now.'

He looked away. 'Yeah, tell me about it.'

Fern was about to ask Alek what he meant when they were interrupted by the same horsey blonde who'd taken her number for Luke. Today the girl was wearing a suit so sharp it threatened to slice into anyone who got too close and had her hair in a neat chignon, but the thin mouth pursed like a cat's bottom was the same.

'Fern Moss? Luke Scottman has a window in his schedule now. He wonders whether you could come over to his trailer?'

'Oh!' Fern's hand fluttered to her mouth. Why did she suddenly feel as though she was on a roundabout and going very fast?

'Like, now?' snapped the PA. 'Mr Scottman's a very busy man.'

'Go on,' Alek said. 'We're done here anyway; they're about to shoot. I'm going to grab some lunch before I move on to the cathedral scene and you deserve a break.'

'Okay.' She kissed him on the cheek, his dark

stubble rasping against her lips. 'I'll catch you and Francesca later.'

Alek held her tightly. 'Be careful,' he whispered into her hair. 'Don't do anything you're not happy with, okay? You've got my number so if you need me just call.'

'Thanks, Al.' Fern hugged him back. 'I'm so lucky to have a friend like you.'

Taking a deep breath to compose herself, she followed the PA's narrow back towards the car park where the production company parked the stars' luxury trailers. Fern could fit her entire flat in one and still have room for Freda's place. It seemed impossible that her Luke, who dropped his socks by the wash bin and who had an unfortunate liking for *Star Trek* was now a bona fide movie star with a trailer all of his own.

Life was weird like that.

And it was about to get a whole lot weirder. Hearing her name called very loudly Fern looked round and her legs turned to damp cotton wool. Surely it couldn't be?

Oh please God, let this be a horrible hallucination, because if it isn't then I really am in trouble.

Standing behind a cordon, separating the trailer park from fans, was Seb.

16

S eb strode across the square as swiftly as the dark storm clouds that were billowing across the pewter sky, after the impatient PR woman beside Fern gave the signal to raise the cordon separating them. His coarse dark curls lifted in the wind and his wide sensual mouth was set in a grim line. Fern's insides knotted like macramé; surely he hadn't flown all the way to Prague just to yell at her for running out on him after their drunken night together?

Okay, she admitted with a prickle of guilt, maybe sneaking out of Seb's flat hadn't been the best course of action. But Seb had never been a man to take no for an answer, so that had seemed a clear way to tell him it was over. Surely he'd understood?

If doing a runner to Eastern Europe wasn't a strong enough hint she was starting to wonder what was.

'It's so good to see you, Fern. You look beautiful,' he said when he reached her. 'But then, you always do.'

Fern was speechless. Shock at seeing him so out of context had frozen her vocal cords. Besides, she was wearing a cat-sick-yellow cagoule, combats and baseball cap and feeling about as unbeautiful as it was possible to ever be. Was Seb having some kind of mid-life crisis?

'I brought you these,' he added, pulling out a large bouquet of red roses from behind his back and flourishing them proudly. Fern took a hasty step backwards, narrowly missing having her eye put out by some lethal thorns. Somehow Seb managed to thrust the velvety blooms into her arms and drop a kiss on her cheek. If Fern hadn't whipped her head round like something out of *The Exorcist* his kiss would have landed smack on her lips.

'What the hell are you doing here?' she demanded at last as irritation restored her powers of speech. 'How come you're in Prague?'

'I've come to see you, of course!' Seb raked a hand through his dark curls. 'I love you, Fern, I keep telling you that. Why did you run out on me? I thought we were back together again.'

Guilt stained Fern's cheeks. 'I'm sorry about that,

Seb. It was really cowardly of me to leave like that. You deserve better.'

He shook his head. 'After what I did I don't deserve any sympathy. Besides, there's no one better than you, angel. If I hadn't messed things up in the first place none of this would have happened. Believe me, if I could turn back time I would. How many times can I swear it'll never happen again?'

Fern sighed. She didn't doubt that Seb was sorry but it frustrated her beyond belief that he couldn't understand why she found it impossible to move on from his fling. Her heart twisted with regret. They'd been happy together, but when she'd found out about Vanessa something deep inside her had shattered. It was only now, three months on and standing in a cobbled square in the watery sunlight, that Fern realised it was her love for him. There was no way she could fix it.

'I want us to be friends as much as you do,' she told him.

'*Friends?* I don't want us to be just *friends*, Fern, that isn't why I had to come and find you. I'm here because I couldn't leave things the way they were. Not after that night we spent together.' His gaze sought hers and Fern knew he was thinking about their lovemaking. 'That night was good, wasn't it?

You and me, we're good together. Come on, Fern. You know we are.'

Fern sighed. Seb had always been good in bed; it was just everywhere else that he was useless. 'It's not enough, Seb. There's got to be more to a relationship than just sex.'

'There's way more to our relationship than sex!' Seb retorted, so loudly that several of the extras drinking coffee by the catering van turned round and stared at them.

'Keep your voice down!' Fern hissed. 'We're *so* not having this conversation here!'

Actually Fern didn't want to have this conversation at all, but if Seb insisted on performing a relationship autopsy at least she could make sure he did it somewhere private.

'Follow me,' she said, taking Seb's elbow and guiding him away from the film crew and along a narrow cobbled side lane which led down to the Vltava.

'Where are we going?'

'Somewhere we can talk alone. I don't want anyone else listening in.'

'Great idea.' Seb gave her a bright smile. 'What did you have in mind? A small boutique hotel somewhere? Don't worry about money, angel. I've got my Amex.'

Fern raised her eyes to heaven. 'I'm not suggesting an afternoon in bed, Seb!'

'That's a shame.' He sighed ruefully. 'So what do you want to do?'

What Fern actually felt like doing was battering him over the head with the roses and then running back to hide in Luke's trailer but instead she took a deep breath. It was time that she laid it on the line and told Seb that she really didn't love him any more.

'Why don't we take a river cruise from the castle and up to the Old Town? It's supposed to be a beautiful way to see Prague.' And hopefully he couldn't cause a scene there either.

'We're going on a sightseeing river cruise?' Seb didn't sound very enthusiastic. 'Wouldn't you rather just grab a bottle of wine and watch the view from the riverbank?'

There was no way Fern was going to let herself get drunk around Seb, not if the last time had set the benchmark. Ignoring his suggestion, she said, 'A friend of Alek's who's a tour guide tells me this boat trip's amazing. I've been meaning to do it all week.'

Tomas had mentioned the trip, although with himself in mind as her companion, and now it seemed like the ideal solution for making sure Seb behaved. Besides, there was still a small part of Fern that didn't trust herself to be alone with Seb. Their passionate history was far too recent for comfort and she still found him incredibly attractive. But on a boat nothing could go wrong, could it?

'I'd rather take you to bed, but I suppose a boat trip might be fun.' Seb's arm snaked round her waist. 'It could be very romantic.'

Fern sidestepped away from his embrace. 'Romance is not on the agenda, okay?'

'Okay,' Seb agreed, but from his smile Fern could tell he didn't believe her for a minute. 'One unromantic boat trip in an unromantic city it is, then!'

They bought their tickets from a small booth beneath a waterlogged striped awning and crossed the gangplank that led towards the stately river cruiser. Couples sat closer than words on the padded seats, to the rear another group of stags were laughing and jostling for the best positions, and a party of schoolchildren were being sorted into regimented rows by their harassed teachers. Excellent, thought Fern. There were plenty of people to ensure Seb behaved himself. What could possibly go wrong?

As the boat slipped away from its moorings Fern settled into her seat at the prow and her taut nerves started to relax. So what if getting on the boat was the emotional equivalent of sticking her head in the sand? At least it was safe. With a sigh of relief she reached into her bag for her guide book, flicking through it until she located the Old Town.

' "The city of spires," ' Seb read over her shoulder, ' "Prague is thought to be one of the most stunning cities in Europe." Well, I won't argue with that. It's beautiful. I wish we'd come here before.'

'*We* haven't come here, Seb.' Annoyed, she snapped the guide book shut. '*I've* come here to visit Alek and Chess. Why *you're* here I really don't know.'

Seb gave her a beady look. 'That's rubbish. You know exactly why I'm here. You've known from the moment you saw me across the square. I'm here because I love you and I want you to come home.'

Fern's heart lurched. 'Seb, I—'

'Shh.' He brushed her lips with his fingers. 'Don't say anything yet. Let me speak. There's so much I want to say to you, lovely, darling Fern, and if you interrupt I'm afraid I might not be able to find the right words.' Seb placed his hands on either side of her face as he spoke. 'I know I messed things up,' he said hoarsely, 'and I know there's nobody to blame but myself, but Fern, you really have to believe me when I say I'm sorry. Not a moment goes by when I don't regret it. I miss you so much. The flat is so quiet without you; it's like living in a tomb. I'm a grumpy bastard at work, I'm miserable at home, I can't eat and I certainly can't sleep.' He gave a harsh laugh. 'Christ! I sound like a corny pop song, but it's true. I'm nothing without you. You make me a better man, Fern. I know I fucked it up, but I need you. I don't think I can be without you.'

She gulped. Nobody had ever said anything like this to her before.

'I made a mistake, babe. Are we both going to pay for it for ever?'

Fern bit her lip. Deep down she knew Seb wasn't a monster – although it had helped her broken heart to tell herself that he was – he was just a normal guy who'd made a mistake. But that mistake, if you could call sleeping with another woman a mistake, was the one thing that she knew she couldn't get over. It would always be in the back of her mind, poisoning her feelings for him.

'You're everything to me,' Seb continued. 'You're the first thought in my mind when I wake up and the last thing I think about when I go to sleep at night. I miss you desperately all the time. I love you, Fern. I really do.'

He looked at her expectantly. This was the part where she was supposed to fling her arms round him and say that she loved him too. Wasn't this what she'd longed for all those endless tearful nights she'd spent howling into her pillow? She'd have died with joy if she'd known that in a few months' time Seb would fly to Prague to tell her he loved her.

They'd been happy together. She'd adored him. So what was stopping her? Fern supposed the bottom line was that she couldn't trust him any more.

'I love you, Fern Moss, and there's only one way that I can prove to you how serious I really am.' Seb slid from the seat to his knees and started rummaging in his jacket pocket. 'I'm never going to let you go again.'

'What are you doing? Seb? Get up!' Even as she said the words Fern had a horrible premonition and her blood turned to iced water. Surely not . . .

'I love you so much,' Seb said desperately, springing open a little box to reveal an enormous diamond solitaire that blinked up at her like an eyeball. 'I can't live without you and I should never have let you go. I was a fool. Fern, will you marry me?'

In an instant Angela's prophecy tightened around

Fern like a vice. The one she'd let go. Was it Seb? How the hell was she supposed to tell?

'Fern, say something! I'm asking you to marry me! You always wanted to get married. Remember all the hints you dropped when Zoe and Steve got engaged?'

'I remember.' Fern's voice was shaky. The eyes of all the other passengers seemed to be focused on them and a sickening wave of adrenaline surged through her bloodstream. Seb was right; at one point she'd wanted to marry him very much. A year ago, when Zoe had shown her her beautiful emerald and diamond engagement ring, Fern had thought she'd combust with envy. But things had been so different back then it was as though she was recalling another life. She'd been head over heels in love with Seb and things had been so perfect between them she'd been convinced he was the one.

But that had been before Vanessa had taken the gloss off her beautiful shiny love affair.

As Seb smiled at her expectantly, offering her the dream that she'd once held so close to her heart, Fern's eyes filled with tears because it was too late. Their relationship was tarnished and broken beyond repair.

There was no way she could marry him.

'What do you say?' pressed Seb. 'I know it's a bit unexpected but I'm asking you to marry me. It's a new start for us both.'

'I'm so sorry, Seb. I can't,' Fern whispered.

'You're saying no?' Seb's eyes were wide with disbelief. 'You're turning me down?'

Everyone on the boat was looking at them now, especially when Seb raised his voice and told Fern loudly that she didn't mean it and was being ridiculous.

'I do mean it!' Fern said. 'And anyway, who's being ridiculous here? We haven't even discussed marriage, Seb. We're not even together any more, so how can we get married? It'd be crazy!'

'You're really saying no?' Seb asked incredulously. He rose to his feet and stepped towards her. 'Come on, you don't mean it. I know you don't!'

'I do!' Fern said, shock at the surprise proposal quickly replaced by annoyance. Seb's inability to listen to her had always been one of the things that had grated. He'd not listened when she'd told him she couldn't get over Vanessa and he certainly wasn't listening now. It was as if he'd applied a Fern filter to his mental programming.

'You're turning me down in front of all these people?' Seb asked. 'Have you any idea how totally humiliating that is for me?'

'This isn't just about you, Seb!' Fern exclaimed, furious with him for putting her in such an awkward situation. 'We haven't discussed anything! As usual you're just assuming what I want without actually bothering to ask me!'

'I'm sorry.' Seb tried to take her hand. 'My timing's crap, but I do love you and I know you love me. Don't you even want to try the ring on?'

Cross, confused and feeling horribly compromised Fern backed away, which was easier said than done in big platform boots on a moving boat. As Seb brandished the enormous ring under her nose and tried to sweep her into his arms she ducked under his arm only to catch her foot in a thick coil of rope. Stumbling and unbalanced, she lurched against the deck's railings. Her arms flailed, trying to clutch at thin air, but unfortunately she was right at the prow of the boat with nothing between her and the river. For a split second she swayed giddily, then gravity took hold and she toppled backwards with a scream, tumbling away from Seb and his glittering ring and into the dark churning waters of the Vltava.

17

The shock of the icy water hit Fern like a punch, blasting the oxygen from her lungs and sucking all sensation from her limbs. Surfacing and gasping for air she heard people shouting, Seb being restrained and life-belts being thrown in, but already the cruise boat had carried on downriver for at least two hundred yards. There was no way she'd ever be able to swim far or fast enough to catch it up.

I'm not even sure I want to make it back to the boat, thought Fern as she struck out for the left bank. *What on earth was Seb thinking, springing a proposal on me like that?* It spoke volumes that she was relieved to find herself swimming in the cold river rather than warm and dry on the boat with Seb and his gigantic engagement ring. Just as well she hadn't accepted; she'd have gone straight to the bottom if she'd been wearing that.

Arms aching and boots heavy with river water, Fern made slow progress. Finally she reached the bank and dragged herself up a flight of stone steps on to the esplanade, collapsing on to a bench to pull off her boots and empty out the water. What a disaster! She couldn't believe what had just happened. Why did she always avoid one scene by creating another? Fern sighed; maybe her mother had a valid point about her dramatic behaviour. After all, how many girls turned down a marriage proposal by hurling themselves off a boat?

Looking on the bright side – which took some doing when you were colder than Frosty the Snowman and smelling like a sewage farm – at least she'd managed to swim to the side of the river where they were filming *Dynamite*. As she wrung out her socks and shook water from her curls Fern saw she was close to a hotel where she and Alek had dressed a scene earlier in the week. If she headed there she could ask reception to call his mobile and ask him or Chess to pick her up. It would be worth having to suffer years of teasing and river jokes to get dry and warm again.

At least she had a plan now. Anything was better than sitting here all soggy and shivering.

Removing a slimy frond of weed from her hair

Fern staggered into the hotel lobby in her bare feet, dripping river water on to the black and white tiled floor. Guests stared, a porter started to smile and one of the immaculate receptionists immediately left her desk and made a beeline for her. Catching a glimpse of her sodden reflection in the beautiful antique mirrors Fern wasn't surprised. She looked terrible, all wild corkscrew curls, combats plastered to her legs and a nose so red that she could double for Rudolph; hardly the usual clientele of the luxurious hotel. She just hoped she'd have time to explain herself before security threw her out or she froze to death.

'Excuse me, madam, but we have a very strict dress code at Hotel Svetlana,' the receptionist told Fern coldly, her delicate nose wrinkling as she caught a whiff of eau de Vltava. 'Perhaps you could return when you're more suitably attired?'

'I'm so sorry, I'm not usually in the habit of falling in the river,' Fern apologised, her teeth chattering so loudly they could have passed as castanets. 'I'm with the film crew for *Dynamite*. Could I please just use your telephone and call my friend?'

The receptionist's nose rose an inch higher into the air. 'I'm sorry, madam, that won't be possible. I believe there's a public telephone outside the hotel.'

'But I haven't got my bag! It's still on the boat. How can I make a call without any money?'

The receptionist shrugged her slim shoulders and with a sinking heart Fern realised that she had no choice but to walk, barefoot and soggy, back to Alek's house. Fan-flipping-tastic. She'd have hypothermia by teatime.

'This way, please,' said the receptionist, indicating the door. 'Or I'll call security.'

'All right, I'm going!' Fern said hastily. God, what a cow! Would it really have damaged the hotel's image beyond repair just to let her use the phone? Trying to muster as much dignity as was possible for a girl soaked to her knickers Fern retraced her steps across the lobby. By now she was shivering like a puppy left outside in a thunderstorm and her feet were turning blue. Surely things couldn't possibly get any worse.

But it seemed they could, for just as she was about to leave the hotel fate decided to flip yet another finger her way.

'Fern? Is that you?' called a deep voice that resonated with masculinity and confidence. 'What the hell happened? Are you okay?'

The hairs on the back of Fern's neck tingled. She knew that voice, as did millions of other people these days. Praying she was wrong, Fern turned round slowly but sure enough there was Luke Scottman, international film star and possibly the most handsome man on the planet, striding across the lobby with his coven of harpies in tow.

No! She didn't want to meet Luke again when she looked like a drowned rat. Maybe if she was really quick she could pretend she hadn't heard him and make a break for it. There was no way she was letting him see her all goose-pimpled and sodden.

'Fern!' Luke doubled his speed. 'It's me! Wait!' Reaching her side he caught her arm and spun her round to face him, but rather than pulling her in for the passionate bone-melting kiss she'd been fantasising about for days he was holding her at arm's length, disbelief etched across his aquiline features. 'Christ! What's happened to you? I was expecting you at my trailer but you never showed up.'

Fern could have howled. Looking like the Thing that crawled in from the Swamp wasn't quite the image she'd dreamed of when meeting up with Luke again. In her mind's eye she'd been wearing her emerald velvet dress and funky Destroy boots, with her hair floating round her shoulders in ringlets and her favourite red heart choker at her throat, full of confidence and more than a match for his blond charisma. Bedraggled and soggy was *so* not a good look. Why oh why did these things always happen to her? Had her parents forgotten to invite the good fairy to her christening or something?

'Your lips are going blue,' continued Luke, horrified. 'Sweetheart, you're frozen! Hey! You there!' He snapped his fingers at the snooty receptionist who'd just given Fern her marching orders. 'Don't stand there gawping! Get this lady a towel!'

'Yes, Mr Scottman!' bleated the receptionist, her heels clacking across the tiles as she raced to do his bidding. Moments later Fern was wrapped in a large fluffy towel while Luke chafed her cold hands between his and ordered a brandy. He was doing an amazing job of warming her up; in fact just touching Luke was enough to raise her temperature to boiling point. He'd always had the most amazing physical presence.

'This is hopeless. You're absolutely soaked!' Luke flung the damp towel back at the glowering receptionist, shrugged off his jacket and draped it round Fern's shoulders. The fabric still held the warmth of his strong muscular body and felt oddly intimate against her chilled skin. 'Spill the beans, Ms Moss. What have you been up to this time?'

She sighed. 'How long have you got?'

He grinned. 'All the time in the world for you, Fern, and I'm more than happy to listen, but we need to get you warmed up first before you die of hypothermia. Jesus, you look like you've been swimming.'

'I have,' she admitted. 'It's a long story, but I was on a boat and ended up falling into the river. I had to swim to the bank.'

Luke's eyebrows shot into his floppy blond fringe. 'Bloody hell, you always were one for dramatics, but falling into the River Vltava is extreme, even for you! No wonder you're frozen. Right, that's it. You're coming up to my suite for a hot bath. Just a bath, Fern,' he added, seeing her hesitate. 'I promise I won't even peep – unless you want me to!'

Luke's glittering blue eyes held Fern's and in spite of being chilled to the marrow she suddenly felt very hot. Luke Scottman had just invited her up to his hotel suite. How was that for a result?

Suddenly things were looking up.

As a lowly set designer Fern had only experienced the kind of luxurious surroundings that Luke was used to when she was actually watching the movies or dressing a set. This huge penthouse suite with carpet so deep the pile was higher than her ankles, a butler to attend to her every need and champagne on tap was like a glimpse of another world. The sheer size of the rooms was incredible. Even the bathroom was at least as large as her flat. As she lay back in a bath scented with Jo Malone bubbles and sipped the vintage Krug Luke had poured for her, Fern reflected that her ex-boyfriend had come a long way since their days at university.

'Do you need anyone to come in and scrub your back?' Luke called from the bedroom, where he was lying on the bed and flicking through the satellite channels. 'You know you want me to!'

'I do not!' Fern laughed, although for a second she was very tempted. Up to her neck in bubbles and with her newly washed hair pinned up in ringlets she felt light years away from the protesting bedraggled creature that Luke had propelled into the lift. On the other hand she also knew of old just what a terrible flirt he could be and she wasn't in any hurry to make even more of an idiot of herself.

'Pity,' sighed Luke. 'Well, let me know if you change your mind.'

Choosing to ignore him Fern sank back into the bath, loving the sensation of the warm silky water against her skin. Feeling like Joan Collins in an episode of *Dynasty* she blew some foam into the air and then tipped some more bath oil into the water. All she needed was a massive pair of shoulder pads and some killer heels waiting for her next to the bath and she'd be right there in 1980s decadence! A girl could certainly get used to this kind of luxury.

'If you wallow in there any more you'll turn into a prune,' Luke warned.

He was right; her hands were already looking decidedly wrinkly. Besides, she could do with a top-up of champagne and there was no way she was going to invite Luke in to pour her a second glass. Wrapping herself in a towel thicker and fluffier than marshmallow she padded across the heated floor in search of her clothes.

At least that was the idea. The only problem was that her clothes seemed to have vanished. Probably Luke's idea of a joke. He'd once hidden all her shoes so that she couldn't go to lectures and had to spend the morning in bed with him. Well, she was wise to his tricks now.

'Where have you hidden my clothes?' she called. 'Come on, Luke, give them back.'

'I haven't hidden them!' Luke protested. 'I got the concierge to take them away and clean them.

They were filthy, remember? I also sent one of my PAs to let your friend know you are okay and to collect your bag when the boat docked – she should be back any minute. Vltava Cruises, wasn't it? And he was called Seb?'

'Well remembered,' Fern called. She suddenly felt guilty that she hadn't thought to let Seb know she was safe. She wasn't sure how he would react to being told that the woman he'd just proposed to was now hanging out with Luke Scottman, an international movie star with a reputation that made Hugh Hefner look like a monk, but she was almost beyond caring. Besides, if Seb hadn't been so arrogant she wouldn't be in this position, would she?

Then a worrying thought occurred. If her clothes had been taken away, what was she going to wear? The thought of being without her clothes in Luke's suite was starting to make her feel on edge and just a little bit vulnerable. Nobody would ever believe it was innocent.

Even she was struggling to believe it was innocent.

'Don't worry, I've already asked the concierge to send up some new ones. You're a size eight, right?'

'Er, that's right.' If she breathed in and wore granny pants. Still, it never hurt to be optimistic.

'He's left a bathrobe here for you too.' Luke

paused and the atmosphere sizzled like frying bacon. 'It's on the bed, though; he must have presumed we're together.'

'Are you in the habit of asking strange women up to your suite and inviting them to take baths?' Fern asked, winding another towel round her damp curls. Then she remembered that this wasn't the Luke she used to know. This was the thirty-something film star version and, if the tabloids were to be believed, asking women up to his hotel suite was *exactly* what Luke Scottman did in his spare time.

'Don't believe everything you read in the papers,' said Luke drily, 'although for your information I don't have to hide girls' clothes any more in order to get them into bed. Anyway, I seem to recall that you didn't used to mind.'

Fern blushed. Knowing that he was thinking about how close they'd once been made the atmosphere pulse with sexual tension. Luke knew every inch of her in the way that only an ex-lover could. He knew she'd loved it when he trailed kisses along her collarbone or nuzzled into the hollow of her throat; he knew a thousand ways to drive her wild. No man is ever seared on to a girl's heart like her first lover and memories of the hopes and dreams they'd once shared broke over Fern in a nostalgic tide.

'I'll pass the robe through the door if you want,' Luke offered. 'I would come in but I don't think the hotel provides chastity belts!'

'I can manage without a chastity belt, thanks. You're not that irresistible!'

'I meant for me, not for you! Chill out, Mossy. I'm offering to fetch you a bathrobe, not asking you to shag my brains out!'

'I doubt that would take very long!' Fern shot back.

'Come out here and say that,' Luke challenged, 'if you dare! And if you want the bathrobe!'

Never one to turn down a challenge, Fern tightened her towel, raised her chin and strode into the master suite to retrieve the bathrobe. At least that was the plan until she caught the corner of the towel in the door. So intent was Fern on reaching the robe that before she realised it the towel had slithered to the floor, leaving her stark naked in the middle of Luke's penthouse.

'Bloody hell, Fern!' Luke almost choked on his Krug. 'What are you trying to do to me?'

18

'Arrgh!' Fern shrieked as she desperately tried to shield her body with her hands. She was so embarrassed she was amazed that she didn't spontaneously combust, leaving nothing but her silver rings and hair slides on the charred carpet. Horrified, she fled back into the bathroom, scooping up the towel and slamming the door behind her, wishing she could drop through the floor. Swaddled in her towel and absolutely mortified, she sat on the side of the bath and buried her head in her hands. What must Luke be thinking? He'd dated some of the most beautiful women on the planet; she was thirty-one and couldn't compete with supermodels even if she lived on air for a month and bathed daily in vats of Crème de la Mer. He'd probably need months in therapy to get over the sight of her wobbly bits.

There was a soft knock at the door. 'I thought you might need this,' said Luke, holding out the bathrobe. He perched next to her on the edge of the bath. 'Although just for the record I think you look even better without it.'

Fern shook her head. 'Don't joke, Luke. I'm too embarrassed.'

'Hey, don't be embarrassed, there's nothing there I haven't seen before. And anyway, I'm not joking. You look fantastic, honestly.' His deep blue eyes twinkled but his famous knicker-melting smile was totally wasted since she wasn't wearing any. Besides, she was far too embarrassed to care about Luke's golden skin touching hers or the closeness of his muscular body.

No, she wasn't thinking about that at all.

'You're lovely, Fern. Every bit as beautiful as I remembered,' Luke said softly. 'I can't believe I lost you. I must have been mad.' He ran a forefinger down her cheek and she shivered. 'You are so gorgeous.'

She bit her lip. 'Yeah, right. Flattery will get you everywhere.'

'Really?' Luke's face lit up like Oxford Street in December. 'Are you going to do the towel thing again?'

'Not like that!' She swatted him on the arm. 'Stop teasing me.'

'Hey, I'm not teasing. In fact I think you're teasing me. Get this robe on right now, young lady, and cover up that sexy body of yours!' Luke bundled it into Fern's arms and then jumped up. 'Don't come back through until you're decent or I won't be responsible for what happens next!'

He pulled a mock leer and Fern laughed. Feeling more at ease – this was only Luke after all and he had a point: he really *had* seen it all before, albeit a long time ago – she indulged herself with the Jo Malone body lotion and then snuggled into the robe. Luke dated models, in fact if the papers were to be believed things were pretty serious between him and Trinity, so he was hardly likely to jump *her* bones; he was just being his old flirtatious self. She had nothing to worry about. Flirting came as naturally to Luke as breathing. If Dot Cotton happened to wander through the suite he'd be chatting her up too.

Safely cocooned in the robe and joining him in the bedroom Fern was surprised and oddly disappointed to find Luke engrossed in an ancient episode of *Star Trek*.

'Hey, come and sit down. Do you remember this

one?' They're stuck on this planet where women rule. Kirk's loving it!' Luke patted the space next to him on the king-sized bed, his eyes not leaving the screen.

'Don't tell me you're still a sad Trekkie?' Fern laughed. Luke had always been a fan of the show and they'd probably watched every episode. She must have really loved him to put up with that.

'It's Trekker actually and there's nothing sad about it. I bet you still blub over *Dirty Dancing*?'

'That's class entertainment!' Fern protested.

'If you say so. Anyway, shush! I think that random crew member in the red jumper is Klingon fodder.'

Curled up on the bed they watched the episode in companionable silence. Once Captain Kirk had saved the universe again Luke cracked open another bottle of Krug and they chatted about university and old friends, laughing at the memories they shared. Outside the penthouse the sky grew dark and shadows slipped across the room, throwing the planes of Luke's face into sharp relief, and mellow with drink and bittersweet nostalgia Fern found herself wondering if they could have made a go of things. They had so much in common and the attraction was still there, she knew. Maybe now they were older and more certain of themselves they could make it work? Stealing a glimpse at him from under her lashes her heart skipped a beat when she caught Luke's gaze seeking hers, his blue eyes bright as gas flames.

'They were good times, weren't they?' he said wistfully. 'Nothing since seems to compare. I sometimes think they were the best days of our lives and we didn't realise it.'

Fern was surprised. 'Aren't you having the best time now? This is what you always wanted, to make it as an actor. It was your dream.'

Luke shrugged. 'It was once but I sometimes wonder. It's a shallow world, Fern, and people only care about what you look like or what you can do for them. I travel so much that it's hard to keep up with my real friends. How's Zoe? She married him then? I heard about the wedding but my schedule's been really hectic.' Luke shrugged helplessly but, for a moment, Fern was touched by the amount of sadness in his eyes. 'If you hadn't turned up in the foyer just now I probably would have found it difficult to make time to see you.'

'Just as well I fell in the river then,' Fern joked, trying to lighten the mood, but Luke remained serious. Deep down there was a lot more to him than the good looks that were all that most people noticed. The only drawback was that his intensity used to cause him to fixate on certain things; his attention to detail probably made him a successful actor but had sometimes been too much for Fern.

'Hey,' she said, nudging him, 'don't look so glum. My God, Luke, you should be over the moon. You've come such a long way since uni. I bet you don't have to re-use sets any more like the old drama society did. Cutting corners like that used to drive you wild, remember?'

Luke gave her a wry smile. 'Was I a total drama queen?'

'Mmm, there was a bit of an Elton John hissy fit when we tried to re-use the set of *Godot* as a wood near Athens!'

Actually, as Fern recalled, *hissy fit* was putting it mildly. Feeling that his artistic integrity was compromised Luke had threatened to walk off the set until Zoe had managed to talk him round. Luke was lucky that Zoe was so patient – Fern had felt like walloping him over the head with a wooden tree. Now, glancing at the beautiful suite where every detail, from the Egyptian cotton sheets to the Green and Black's organic chocolate, was perfect, Fern suspected that Luke was still every bit as demanding.

'Do you make your assistants sort your M and M's into colour-coded bowls as well?' she teased.

'Now there's a thought!' Luke raised an eyebrow. 'I don't suppose you fancy a job, do you? I don't eat the—'

'Orange ones! I know!' Fern laughed. 'How could I forget? Didn't I always have to eat the orange Jelly Babies for you, and Opal Fruits too? Jeez! There's not enough money in the world to persuade me to take that job on. Besides, I know all your worst habits, remember?'

'There's nothing like an old friend to put a guy firmly back in his place,' Luke said.

'Less of the old, thanks! Let me point out that I'm eight months younger than you.'

'And you look bloody fantastic too. It's so good to see you, Fern. It makes uni feel like yesterday, doesn't it?'

Fern nodded. 'My mother always says there are no friends like old friends.'

'Too right.' Luke's voice was hoarse. 'And we're really old friends, aren't we? In fact, there was a time when we were more than friends. Much more,' he said huskily. 'I always loved your dramatic streak. That fire about you and all that passion is so damn sexy. Christ, Fern, I want you.'

The atmosphere crackled like Space Dust and the room seemed to slip out of focus. His hand rose to cup her face. 'Oh, Fern, I've missed you,' he whispered.

The passion in his voice and the bitter-sweet memories broke over her like a tidal wave. When Luke leaned forward and kissed her, a soft and sweetly familiar kiss, Fern closed her eyes and kissed him back. It was a kiss that grew deeper and more questioning as his hands slipped beneath her robe and followed the curve of her breast. He was every bit as gorgeous as she remembered and for a nanosecond Fern felt like flinging caution to the wind and just giving in to the desire that was burning through her bloodstream like magma. Luke was so achingly familiar. Surely it wouldn't hurt?

As she pulled the T-shirt over his head she gasped because his body was incredible. Strong broad shoulders, arms sculpted with muscle and just a fine sprinkling of blond hair which tapered over a six-pack stomach and down to his belt. An impressive erection strained against the fabric of his jeans and as Luke pulled her on top of him she moaned with need, wrapping her legs around him and winding her fingers into his thick honey-coloured hair. Every inch of her skin was on fire, every cell quivering with desire.

Luke's lips strayed to her collarbone. 'You've not changed at all, Fern. You're every bit as sweet now as you always were.'

Sweet? Alarm bells started to trill in Fern's mind. She wasn't sweet. She was a woman and thirty-one years old, not the shy, mop-headed little student he'd dated all those years ago. Of course she'd changed.

Luke's right hand cupped her breast and she felt his erection nudge her thigh. His eyes were closed, as though lost in some long-ago memory, and Fern started to feel uneasy. Nostalgia sex was probably right up there with revenge sex and mercy sex when it came to bad ideas.

'I feel so comfortable with you,' he was murmuring. 'Oh, Fern, you knew me, the real me, way before all this fame crap started. You're so safe and familiar.'

Familiar? Safe? These were hardly the words to turn a girl on or to make her feel like a goddess in the sack. Fern felt the excitement that had been crackling through her nervous system pop away for good.

Safe and *familiar*? Was this how Luke saw her? Some kind of nostalgic comfort blanket to keep him grounded? The irony of this almost made Fern laugh out loud. *She* was the one who needed someone to keep *her* feet firmly on the floor. He didn't know her at all if that was what he thought.

'Oh, Fern,' Luke groaned. 'You're gorgeous. I want you so much.' Then he was slipping the bathrobe from one shoulder and kissing the soft skin of her throat, while one hand moved across her breast, her nipple hardening under his fingertips. As his lips moved even lower and she found her hands scrabbling to undo his belt Fern knew this was a kiss that could only end one way.

She'd been that way before. Was she sure that she really wanted to go there again? If she did she'd be giving Luke a very clear message. She fancied him like crazy, she wanted nothing more than to give in to the delicious sensations marauding through her body, but did she love Luke? Was he the one? What if he said the word? Was she really ready to give up her life to follow him around from location to red carpet event to Hollywood mansion? She hadn't wanted that lifestyle ten years ago; what had changed that she'd want it now?

And what about Alek's job offer? If you're seeing Luke you'll never get to work with Al. Suddenly it was as though someone had thrown a bucket of iced water over her and her hands fell away from Luke's boxers.

'We can't do this.' She broke the kiss, as breathless as though she'd just swum across the Vltava again.

'Of course we can!' Luke said quickly. 'We're both adults. You want me and I definitely want you, as you can probably tell. What's to stop us? Can't we just pretend that time's stood still? I'm not asking you to stay for ever, Fern. I'm just asking you to stay tonight.' He reached out and took her hand in his. 'I'm just asking you to keep me company.'

'Luke, I can't.' She pulled her hand away. 'I'm so sorry, but this feels wrong.'

'It doesn't feel wrong to me,' he insisted. 'Just one night, for old times' sake? To remember how we used to be, perhaps?' He gave her the winning Luke Scottman smile. 'Come on, aren't you just the tiniest bit tempted?'

Although she went to a Catholic school Fern had never claimed to be a saint. Of course she was tempted. Seriously tempted. Luke was gorgeous, wealthy beyond her wildest imaginings, and from a purely shallow point of view being desired by a movie star was a major boost to an ego that Seb had so recently stomped his size tens all over. She was only a pulse away from making love to Luke. Slipping out of her robe and letting him continue would be the easiest, nicest thing in the world. But would it be the right thing?

And then and there, with the robe sliding off her shoulders and her lips pink and swollen from kissing, Fern had a sudden epiphany. Luke wasn't her soulmate, the one she'd let go. They were light years apart. Luke was a lovely guy but being here with him wasn't real, it was just a fantasy, a way to escape the reality of the mess she'd made of things with Seb and Matt while pretending to be eighteen again.

'Luke, you're an amazing guy, but—'

'Christ, stop analysing it!' Luke sat up, his eyes bright with frustration. 'Just relax, Fern.'

She pulled her robe together and drawing her knees against her chest wrapped her arms around them. 'This is a bad idea, Luke. I'm a mess at the moment. I don't know what I want and you deserve better than that. It's not—'

Luke rolled away from Fern, crossing his arms behind his head and staring up at the ceiling. 'Why do I get the feeling I'm about to be given the brush-off?'

Fern pressed the heels of her hands against her eyes. Turning down a gorgeous movie star while lying almost naked on his king-sized bed wasn't something that happened to her every day and quite frankly it was very annoying, rather like winning the lottery and then developing a spending allergy. What was it with the men in her life at the moment? Talk about buses arriving all at once. She was in danger of getting run over. It would all have been very flattering if the men involved actually wanted *her*, but Fern was realistic and honest enough to know that she wasn't that irresistible. If only! No, Seb had an ego the size of the moon and saw her rejection of him as a challenge, and Luke only wanted a one-way ticket down memory lane. Neither guy really wanted *her*.

And, if she were totally honest, she didn't want them either.

She sighed. 'Luke, this is a bad idea. Really, it isn't me you want. You just want to turn the clock back and feel eighteen again.'

'Is that such a bad thing? Things were less complicated then, weren't they? You, me and Zoe, we were all such good friends.'

He looked so sexy, all rumpled on the bed with his toned stomach revealed, that she almost weakened. Why oh why couldn't she have had her epiphany *after* they'd slept together?

'We're not eighteen any more,' Fern said gently.

'We're not the same people. And aren't you seeing someone? It makes everything very complicated, as does the army of paps camped outside the hotel. This is nothing like being freshers, Luke. Surely you can see that? And anyway, why would you want to go back when you've got everything you ever wanted?'

Luke sighed and swung his long, lean body from the bed. Walking slowly to the French windows he leaned his forehead against the glass and stared out at the twinkling lights of Prague.

'What makes you think I've got everything I want? All the money? The fame?' He shook his blond head. 'My life's hard to explain, Fern. Some parts are fantastic but there's a high price to pay and most of the time it's like being a bloody prisoner. I can't tell you just how good it is to talk to someone who sees through all that movie star bollocks.' His shoulders sagged. 'I suppose I thought that for once it would have been nice to make love to someone who knew the real *me* rather than Luke bloody Scottman the film star. Even I'm sick of him.'

Fern said nothing because there was no answer to that. Luke's road was a lonely one and her heart went out to him, but sleeping with her wasn't the answer to whatever it was that was making him so unhappy. Whatever – whoever – Luke was looking for she knew that she wasn't it.

'I'm sorry, Luke,' she said helplessly. 'I shouldn't have come up here. It was a bad idea.'

'I'm still glad you did,' he said. 'And I'm sorry if I jumped to the wrong conclusion when I assumed that you'd ... well, you know. I think I've been suckered into believing my own publicity. I guess we've both moved on since uni. Maybe you're right, and we're not the same people we used to be.'

Fern placed a hand on his arm. 'We had a great time though, didn't we?'

'We had the best time. How did it all end up like this?'

Luke reached out and took Fern's hand. Fingers laced tightly together they shared a kiss, a gentle kiss, and pulled apart.

Feeling suddenly awkward in the robe Fern dressed swiftly in the clothes left by the concierge and scooped up her bag while Luke called the private lift. As the doors hissed shut the last thing she saw was his heart-stopping smile, blurring and dancing as her eyes swam with tears. Then the lift glided downwards taking her away from Luke Scottman and any hopes she'd cherished.

How was that for crap timing? It was just her

luck. Not that for a second she'd really seen herself as the consort of a Hollywood star. She was about a foot too short and several stone too wide for that but still, a girl could dream. With a sigh, Fern waited for the lift doors to open, her new outfit of a floaty pink dress, tan Mary Janes with a vivid red sole and a cream crochet cardigan far more in keeping with the elegant décor than the drowned rat look of earlier. Even if she would have never chosen the outfit herself Fern decided that whoever ended up with Luke would be a lucky and well-dressed girl.

It just wouldn't be her.

Stumbling out of Luke's private lift half blinded by tears, Fern was rather taken aback to discover Seb waiting for her in the foyer.

Shit. Seb. Bloody hell, what do you say to a man whose proposal you've just turned down?

'Here, one large white wine.' Seb joined Fern on a low sofa, taking care to leave as much space between them as possible, and took a big slug of his lager.

Not wanting to publicly destroy Seb's ego in a hotel lobby, Fern had suggested they go somewhere to talk things through. Ten minutes later, they'd wandered down a cobbled street and found a quiet bar.

'So,' Seb said eventually. 'If you didn't jump into the Vltava to avoid agreeing to marry me does that mean there's still a chance for us?'

Fern winced at the hope in his voice. Reluctant to hurt him but knowing she had absolutely no choice but to make her feelings plain she shook her head. 'I'm sorry, Seb, but I can't marry you. It would never work between us. It's over.'

Seb stared at her in amazement, as though she'd just informed him that the earth was flat. 'You don't mean that. You love me, I know you do.'

Now it was Fern's turn to take a huge swig of her drink. Not that the alcohol would help much, unless she could drink enough to turn her teeth numb and then slither unconscious to the floor, but she badly needed some Dutch courage. Or should that be Czech courage? Short of wearing a sandwich board with *It's Over Seb!* painted on it the only way to get the message through was to be blunt.

'I don't love you any more, Seb,' she said quietly.

'You're being ridiculous,' Seb snapped. 'This is your way of punishing me for what happened with Vanessa, isn't it? Christ, Fern, I'm sorry, okay? Can't we change the record? People make mistakes.'

Fern's blood started to boil as though somebody had stuck a Bunsen burner under her backside, but she tried to remain calm. 'Maybe the Vanessa thing was just a symptom of things not working out between us. Perhaps you'd be better off with someone like her.'

'I don't want to be with bloody Vanessa!' He grabbed her hands so tightly that she yelped. 'Fern, I don't want to be with Vanessa. It's you I love and want to marry. Please don't be stubborn and let a few stupid slip-ups ruin our relationship. Things will be great between us again, I swear it. They'll be even better than before!'

Fern's blood went from boiling to ice water in a split second. The noise in the bar ceased as though someone had pressed mute and there was a hideous rushing sound in her ears. Wait a minute. What the hell did he mean by *a few* stupid slip-ups? Just how many times *had* he slept with Vanessa?

She snatched her hands away as though afraid of being contaminated. 'How many times did you actually screw her? And don't lie to me. You've already admitted it was more than once.'

Seb grimaced. 'Christ, Fern, does it matter? I'm not asking Vanessa to marry me so there's nothing to be jealous of. Why do we have to go over all this again?'

'I'm going over it because it's important to me to know how many times my lying, cheating ex-partner chose to shag that slapper! How many times? I need to know, Seb! How can I possibly marry you if you can't be honest with me?'

Lord, that felt good, like releasing an emotional valve.

Seb pinched the bridge of his nose and blew heavily through his nostrils as though he was trying to snort out the guilt. 'Okay, babe, you want me to be honest? Fine, I'll be honest, but please believe me when I say I regret every minute I spent with her. It was never about you. I was lonely.' A sulky expression clouded his face. 'You were always bloody working. What was I supposed to do?'

'Not shag someone else!'

Not for the first time Fern really resented the smoking ban. Not because she wanted a fag – smoking all the time, like being with Seb, was a habit she was glad to have broken – but because she would have loved to beat the truth out of him with a heavy ceramic ash tray.

'How many times?'

Seb shrugged. 'Five? Maybe six? You were away a lot, babe, filming *Jane* and seeing your family. I guess I got lonely.' He tried to give her his winning smile but to Fern it just looked like a smirk. 'I'm a normal guy, Fern, and I have needs. So I messed up. I'm sorry.'

'Because you're a man you can screw around?' Now Fern's hackles were well and truly up. 'How the hell do you figure that out?'

'Christ! This is all coming out wrong!' Seb thumped the table in annoyance, slopping their drinks over the sticky surface. 'I'm trying to explain why it happened. I know I cocked up. I know I was an idiot but I really, really am sorry. Why won't you believe me? I really do love you, babe.' His voice went on and on, but Fern could think of only one thing.

'Six times?' She was staggered. Not even Carol Vorderman could work that equation out.

'No! It isn't like that. Vanessa is nothing like you. She was just there,' Seb cried.

'She's a person with feelings, not bloody Everest!'

'I know! I know! I messed up and it's entirely my fault. But I've been desperate to make it up to you and win you back. I even started following you just so that I could see you again.' He tried to peer upwards through his lashes in a winning Princess of Wales manner but only succeeded in doubling Fern's longing for a blunt object to wallop him with. 'That was why I was outside the fancy-dress party that night. I knew you were there and I was waiting for you.'

'You were stalking me?'

His eyes narrowed with annoyance. 'Why do you have to twist everything I say?'

'I don't need to listen to any more of this.' Leaping to her feet Fern decided that she wasn't going to pollute her ears for another second. 'I don't love you and I never will so please, please won't you push off back to England!'

Seb's mouth opened and closed and he looked like a goldfish dressed by Paul Smith as he struggled to reply. 'But what will I do without you?' he said finally. 'What will I do on my own?'

'They look keen,' Fern said coolly, pointing at a group of hens who now were playing a rowdy drinking game and leering at the barman. They were all raucous laughter and L-plates as they spilled in from the street and Fern found herself wishing that Zoe had gone for this approach. Booze and fun would have been a million times better than the ridiculous fortune-telling idea and probably a lot less trouble too. Since Angela had read her cards Fern's life had taken more twists and turns than Spaghetti Junction. 'I'm sure you won't be alone for long. Christ, it seems I couldn't even leave you alone for a weekend without you finding another woman to play with. So, happy hunting!'

And with that parting shot Fern slammed down her empty glass and stormed out of the bar, leaving Seb all alone with his ring and his regrets. She felt a flash of white-hot anger when she recollected just how much emotion she'd wasted on him and the whole prophecy business.

Well, not any more. It was time to make some changes . . .

'Fern! Are you okay?' Alek pulled up in a sleek Mercedes and flung the passenger door open for Fern. 'My God, have you been crying? Whatever happened with Luke Scottman?'

'Luke?' For a second Fern was confused. Her afternoon with Luke felt a million light years ago. Instead the conversation with Seb kept replaying on a nasty little loop. How could he have thought she wouldn't be upset that he'd slept with Vanessa more than once? What sort of person was he? And what sort of an idiot was she to have been taken in by him for so long?

After shouting at Seb Fern had stormed into the street where she'd gulped great lungfuls of cool night-time air and forced herself not to cry. Still consumed with anger but feeling slightly more in control she'd followed another raucous hen party into a wine bar and bought the biggest glass of Chardonnay possible, short of ordering the bottle and necking it.

Bloody great. Now Seb was driving her to drink.

But the more Fern drank the angrier she felt. How dare Seb brush his infidelity under the carpet and then expect her not to feel any worse that he'd slept with Vanessa more than once? He could bleat on all he wanted about its still being the same woman and only counting as one mistake but it certainly didn't feel like that to Fern, and with every excuse that slipped from his lips she'd felt worse. Sleeping with another woman wasn't like eating one biscuit and then guzzling the contents of the entire tin because now the diet was broken so sod it! But by the time she was through her second glass Fern had moved on from anger to despair and was ready to drown herself in the wine glass.

Death by Chardonnay it was then. She supposed there were worse ways to go.

But this plan was quickly thwarted when Fern discovered she was out of money. She'd left all her credit cards safely at Alek's, in a desperate attempt to try to resist all the amazing shops that Prague laid before her like consumerist confectionery. She didn't even have enough for a taxi so, admitting defeat, she called Alek and asked if he could pick her up. Ever the loyal friend, Alek just asked for the name of the bar and promised he'd be there as quickly as possible. Now, as she eased her aching body into the car, Fern thought she'd never been more pleased to see him. Her arms hurt from the long swim and her heart was sore from the knife wounds of Seb's infidelity. Once she was back at Alek's Fern had every intention of drinking herself into oblivion.

Alek took one look at her pale face and was horrified. 'Fern, you're worrying me. What's happened? What did he do? If he hurt you I swear to God, action hero or not, I'll kill him.'

'What?' Fern surfaced from her doom-laden thoughts like a diver surfacing from the deep.

'Luke Scottman. You were off to see him when I last saw you,' Alek reminded her as the car glided into the traffic.

Fern was puzzled. What had Luke got to do with Seb's inability to keep it in his trousers? 'Luke?'

'Movie star? A bit like Brad Pitt's better-looking brother?'

'Oh, right. Luke.' Fern ground her knuckles into her eyes and yawned. Her time with Luke felt as though it had happened to someone else. 'Yeah, we met up but there's nothing between us. We're just friends.'

'That's good, yes?' Alek's gaze was fixed on the road ahead. Stealing a glance across at him Fern thought how square and strong his jaw was; he always reminded her of a hero from one of her favourite old black and white movies. She was lucky to have this honest and dependable guy as her friend. She knew he'd never let her down.

Alek's eyes met hers and he smiled gently. 'Or maybe it isn't good? You don't seem very happy about it. Were you hoping Luke would be the love of your life?'

'No, I'm fine about it.' And she was too, she really was. 'Luke's a nice guy but we live totally different lives now. Honestly, you should have seen his suite, Alek! It was like something out of *Footballers' Wives*. We've not got anything in common.'

Alek laughed. 'Then perhaps we should be glad that you can draw a line under that relationship. I can't really see you with a Tango tan and wearing a pink velour track suit. And the six-inch acrylic nails wouldn't be very practical for set design.'

'It's more like Tiffany necklaces and Versace in Luke's world,' Fern mused. 'Anyway, like I said, things with Luke are cool. It's Seb who's caused problems today.'

'Seb? How does he come into it?' Alek changed lanes swiftly, one strong hand looped over the gear stick. Fern loved the way he drove, fast but with a quiet confidence. She always felt safe when Alek was behind the wheel, not like the churning terror she'd suffered when out with Seb, who drove like Lewis Hamilton on speed, with the vocabulary of Gordon Ramsay thrown in for good measure.

'Seb turned up in Prague this afternoon,' Fern said. 'He proposed to me.'

'He did what!' Alek's jaw was almost on the dashboard. Pulling the car to the side of the road he killed the engine and turned to stare at her. 'I can't listen to this and drive. I'm only a guy!'

She laughed. 'Yeah, sorry. I forgot the multi-tasking thing. To cut a long and very awkward story short, just after I left you Seb appeared, armed with most of the red roses in Czechoslovakia, and declared undying love for me.'

'After all he'd done? What a bloody nerve!' Then a horrified expression flashed across Alek's mobile features. 'Christ, you didn't accept his proposal, did you?'

'Of course I didn't!'

'Phew.' Alek mimed mopping his brow. 'Thank God for that. So, what happened?'

'Now this really is a long story involving proposals, a swim across the Vltava and revelations of infidelity,' she sighed. 'Fancy discussing it over a bottle of wine?'

Alek checked his Rolex. 'I'm supposed to be

eating with Francesca's family. Her sister Christina just announced her engagement so there's a full-on celebration taking place, but this sounds far more interesting.'

'Oh, Alek! You left a family engagement party to come and pick me up?' Fern felt awful. 'I'm so sorry. I should have walked back. Just drop me at home and go back now!'

He pulled a face. 'It's a bit too much, to be honest, and there's only so much wedding talk a man can take. Chess isn't happy either that her sister's got engaged first, so I was pleased to get a break. Besides, what else are friends for?'

'You've got to go straight back to the engagement party,' Fern insisted. There was already tension between Alek and Chess and she certainly didn't want to make things worse. 'I don't want to get in the way.'

Alek crossed his arms and shook his head. 'I think not, Ms Moss! Not until I hear all about what you've been up to and no leaving out any details. I need to hear everything. Yes?'

Fern knew from experience that once Alek made his mind up there was no arguing with him. Unlike Luke, who could always be persuaded to another way of thinking – usually thanks to Zoe who seemed to have a knack for smoothing his ruffled feathers –

Alek knew his own mind and no one could sway him. It was what made him such a good business-man and such a devoted friend.

So settling back into the cream leather seat she told Alek all about the crazy events of the after-noon. Alek was a good listener. He never inter-rupted or judged; now he just nodded or shook his head and, when she started to cry again as she recounted Seb's confession that he'd slept with Vanessa five or six times, handed her a freshly laundered hanky.

'Sorry,' Fern sniffed, blotting her eyes with the crisp cotton. 'I can't believe I'm still so upset. It's not as though I wanted to marry Seb, is it? And I already knew he'd cheated on me so that's hardly a surprise either.'

Alek put his arm round her shaking shoulders and pulled her against him. 'He's a shit, Fern. You're worth a thousand of him.'

'But why did he cheat on me? Wasn't I good enough?'

'He cheated on you because he's inadequate and pathetic.' Alek's brow was creased with anger as he tenderly wiped her tears away with his thumb. 'Honestly, Fern, what Seb did hasn't got anything to do with you. You're funny and talented and gorgeous.

Any man would be over the moon to be with someone like you.'

'Yeah, right.'

His arm tightened round her shoulder. 'It's their loss, Fern. I'm so sorry you haven't found the answer you wanted in Prague. Perhaps you should take some time out? After all, what's the urgency?'

Fern blew her nose. Thank God she wasn't trying to impress Alek. Bloodshot eyes and a snotty nose were so not an attractive look.

'If I tell you will you promise not to laugh?' She crumpled the hanky in her hand. It was all sodden and creased, a bit like her.

'I'd never laugh at you,' Alek promised. 'You can tell me anything, you know that.'

Fern took a deep breath and out tumbled the story of Zoe's hen night and Angela's prophecy. 'I know it sounds crazy,' she finished, 'but too much of what she said was true for it to just be a coincidence. Do you think I'm mad?'

Alek exhaled slowly. 'I've never been one for psychic phenomena but I know a lot of people who do set a great deal of store by that kind of thing. I wouldn't be so arrogant as to rule anything out. There's got to be more to life than we can see.'

'That's exactly what I think!'

Alek held up a hand to stop her. 'On the other hand I don't like the idea that our entire lives are all planned out for us and nothing we do will make any difference. The concept of fate horrifies me. I'd much rather make my own destiny.'

'But that's what I am doing!' Fern cried. 'I let the love of my life go so I'm going to change fate by finding him again. I'm getting there. So far I've ruled out two of the three.'

Alek looked puzzled. 'Who's left?'

'Matt.' Fern uncurled her hand and looked down at her mobile phone. She had two missed calls from him. Although he'd not left a message she couldn't help feeling the fact that he'd called was significant. Frustratingly, just as she tried to call him back the battery died. Now she was frantic to know what he wanted.

'The vet?'

Fern's brain started to whirl like a Catherine wheel. It was a faint chance but still a chance none the less that Matt could be the one. He was honest and true and she knew he still had feelings for her. Had he been working his feelings through all this time while she, impatient as always, had read it as a rejection? After all, she'd made it more than clear that she wouldn't see any man who was attached, and similarly Matt would never cheat on someone. Had she jumped to the wrong conclusion yet again?

Alek said nothing but stared into the velvet-black night, all beaded with necklaces of ruby tail-lights and diamond headlamps.

'There's still a chance,' murmured Fern, more to herself than to Alek. 'It could be Matt, don't you think?'

'I suppose so,' Alek agreed, but he didn't sound very enthusiastic about continuing the discussion. 'But if it isn't and you discover that you've ruled him out too then my job offer still stands. It will always stand.'

But even as Alek spoke, Fern hardly heard his words because her imagination was cranked up into fifth gear and excitement was fizzing through her bloodstream like sherbet. There was no way she was going to start a new life in Prague now; in fact she wasn't even sure that she could stay a minute longer.

Was Matt the one that she'd let go?

The more she thought about it the more Fern was starting to think he could be.

And there was only one way to find out.

20

Two days later Fern unlocked her front door, sighing with relief to be back home again. Filled with optimism, it had taken every drop of self restraint Fern possessed not to call Matt from Alek's. Patience had never been one of her virtues – Cybil had always been driven to distraction trying to find new and increasingly ingenious places to hide her Christmas presents – but she'd told herself that this was a conversation that she and Matt had to have face to face. Alek hadn't said much about this idea, but following his swift exit from the engagement party things had seemed rather cool between him and Francesca and Fern had understood that he had his own issues to deal with.

Prague had been a lovely break and she had every intention of going back and visiting, but right now it was really good to be home. From the moment her plane had touched down on the wet Heathrow tarmac she'd been dying to charge up her mobile and call Matt. She'd make some coffee to give the phone time to charge, and hopefully by then she'd have figured out exactly what to say . . .

Kicking a pile of junk mail out of the way and dragging her zebra-print wheelie case behind her Fern burst into the hallway. The flat was still and had the watchful air of somewhere that had been shut up for a while. A layer of dust had settled on the table and the rubber plant was gasping for a drink. Radio 4 chattered through the party wall from Freda's house while on the other side of the hallway one of the Sandhus' brood thudded down the stairs. Although there was none of the elegance of Alek's townhouse and the grey roofs of Tooting were a far cry from the soaring spires of Prague, it was still home and she was pleased to be back.

Fern scooped up her post before wandering into the kitchen and filling the kettle. Moments later she'd kicked off her knee-length biker boots and curled up on the sofa with her mobile charging and her laptop booting up so she could check her emails. Now that she was only seconds away from speaking to Matt Fern was starting to feel nervous. He was engaged, after all. Was she being as bad as Vanessa by deliberately seeking out a man she knew was with someone else? And did that make Matt as bad as Seb? It wasn't a comfortable comparison.

Fern closed her eyes wearily. The mental gymnastics were wearing her out. Since when had everything become so complicated?

It was the sound of her mobile ringing that woke her. For a second she was totally disorientated. Images of Seb chasing her with a giant ring were still dancing through her mind as she fumbled for her handset and knocked cold coffee all over her jeans.

'Oh shit!' she wailed, desperately trying to mop the liquid up with her junk mail. 'Bollocks! Bum!'

'That's a charming way to answer the phone,' said a warm voice. 'I take it you're less than pleased to hear from me?'

It was Matt. Fern sat bolt upright, all traces of sleep banished instantly as monster hits of adrenaline zoomed round her nervous system like hormonal quad bikes.

'Matt! Hi! Sorry about that. I'd just nodded off and I've knocked my coffee over. It's no reflection on you, honestly. I've just got back from Prague and I'm really tired.'

Catching sight of her reflection in the hall mirror,

Fern pulled a face. Tired didn't even come close. She could put a week's shopping in the bags under her eyes and her hair looked like something from a Dulux advert. Thank goodness she didn't use Skype!

'Did you have fun?' Matt asked.

Now there was a question. She'd fallen in the river, snogged an international film star and received a marriage proposal, but had she had fun? No, you'd have to be twisted to find any of that fun.

'It was certainly interesting,' she said thoughtfully. 'I'm very glad to be home now, though.'

'I'm glad you're home too.' Matt's voice was low. 'Listen, Fern, I've been thinking a lot about what happened the last time I saw you and I'm not proud of the way I left things.' He paused and she could hear him drumming his fingers on a table top, a sure sign of stress. 'I should have called you sooner. I'm really sorry.'

Fern closed her eyes. 'So why didn't you?'

He exhaled slowly. 'Come on, Fern. You know why. Everything's so complicated.'

'You mean you got cold feet,' Fern said gently. 'It's okay, Matty, you're not the only one. I guess I was a bit freaked out too. Nothing's as straightforward as it used to be, is it?'

'You can say that again,' Matt said with feeling.

'It's not that I don't want . . . that I didn't mean . . .'

'Shh,' Fern said. 'I understand.'

She thought of Luke and how easy it would have been to have got swept away by him so she could hardly blame Matt, especially since she'd deliberately sought him out. Looking back she felt really bad about that. Disrupting Matt's life on a whim had been selfish and not something that she was proud of.

'Maybe.' Matt didn't sound convinced. 'Look, Fern, you can say no if you like but do you think we could meet? I know it sounds crazy but I really need to see you.'

'You want to see me? When?'

'Are you free this evening? Or is that too soon?' Matt sounded nervous. 'Shall I wait until tomorrow? I don't want to but I will if you'd rather.'

'No, no, tonight's fine,' said Fern, trying to stop herself from doing a Tom Cruise on the sofa. 'Shall I drive over to yours?'

'Absolutely not. I won't hear of it,' he said firmly. 'You've done quite enough travelling for one day. I'll come over to you. Is half eight okay?'

'Half eight sounds perfect,' Fern told him, thanking her lucky stars that she'd tidied up before going to stay with Alek.

'Great. I'll see you soon,' Matt said and she could hear the smile in his voice. Once he'd rung off Fern sat on the sofa and stared at her mobile. What on earth had happened to make him so keen to see her all of a sudden? Maybe he'd called things off with Amanda and was coming over to tell her? At this thought she hugged her fluffy red cushion to her chest and tried to control her nerves. Was that really what she wanted? Her knees turned to water.

She checked her watch. Only fifty minutes until Matt arrived! Whatever he wanted she wasn't going to meet him with dirty hair and travel-creased clothes. Jumping to her feet she swept her junk mail into the bin, switched on the lamps and fluffy fairy lights and shoved a bottle of sparkling wine into the fridge. Then she showered and dressed quickly, rubbing sparkly vanilla body lotion all over herself, blasting her curls dry and pulling them into a high ponytail. Tinted moisturiser and a few blobs of Touche Eclat took care of her pallid skin, and with a sweep of mascara her blue eyes sparkled back at her as though she was already halfway through the Cava. Her cheeks were pink with excitement and putting on lipstick seemed a pointless activity since Matt was only going to kiss it all off, so she settled for a slick of Benetint lipgloss instead. Rummaging through her underwear drawer Fern rooted out a sweet pink and white candy-striped set that she'd been given by Cybil and never worn, preferring her usual bright oranges and hot pinks. But Matt was a more traditional kind of guy and had always liked Fern to look girly. She paused for a second before stepping into the knickers and snapping the bra on. Who was she to deny Matt after all this time? The set was frilly and scratchy but he was worth it! Twirling in front of her mirror to check her reflection, Fern then pulled on her favourite vintage Levi's and a strawberry-pink sweatshirt and slipped her small feet into glittery flip-flops. Just as she was contemplating painting her toenails to match her sweater the doorbell shrilled.

Matt had arrived.

Fern's mouth dried. This was really it. Angela's prophecy was about to be fulfilled.

Running down the stairs, her ponytail bouncing in time with every step, Fern threw open the door and there was Matt in his beloved jeans and Barbour jacket, shuffling from foot to foot and looking so nervous that her heart went out to him. She flung her arms round his neck. She couldn't wait for him to hold her close. Good old dependable Matt was the antithesis of Seb and that made him totally right for her. Why had she been so stupid and not realised earlier?

'Oh, Matty, it's so good to see you!' she cried, giving him a quick hug. 'Come in.'

'It's good to see you too.' Matt hugged her back and then followed her into the hall where he shrugged off his heavy coat. 'I really wish I'd called you earlier but I've been so confused.'

'You and me both,' Fern admitted. 'I think we've got some serious talking to do, don't you?'

He nodded. 'I've been trying to work out what it is that I want to say for weeks now but every time I think I've figured it out I change my mind. You have the strangest effect on me, Fern. I think maybe you always did.'

His expression was so serious and his brown eyes so earnest that Fern suddenly felt like she wanted to ruffle his hair and tell him that everything was going to be okay. Mmm. Hardly the most lover-like of responses. Shouldn't she be desperate to rip his clothes off rather than wanting to mother him? Figure that out, Freud!

Matt perched on the edge of the sofa. Putting his nervousness down to being close to her Fern plopped on to a bean bag and drew her knees up against her chest. 'What's wrong?' she asked. 'You weren't this uptight the last time I saw you.'

Matt's fists were clenched so tightly that his knuckles glowed white through his flesh. Then he took a deep breath and turned to face her. 'Look, Fern, I behaved really badly that day. I wasn't fair to you and I certainly wasn't fair to Amanda.' He closed his eyes wearily. 'I haven't been able to stop thinking about what almost happened between us, what would have happened if you hadn't had the good sense to tell me to think carefully about what I really wanted.'

Fern didn't say anything but discovered that she was holding her breath. This didn't sound like the preamble to a declaration of undying love, more like the prelude to a thanks but no thanks speech. She recognised the tone. It was the same one that she'd used with Luke. For a second Fern thought about interrupting and telling him that actually she really regretted encouraging him to go but Matt wasn't in the mood to listen. Instead he was ploughing on with a speech he'd obviously written earlier.

'You're an amazing girl, Fern, and I haven't been able to stop thinking about you since Zoe's wedding.' He slipped from the sofa to kneel by her side. Reaching out, he took her small hands in his large strong ones and gazed into her eyes with such burning intensity that she almost expected her eyeballs to sizzle. 'When I told you that I never stopped loving you I wasn't lying.'

'I know,' she whispered. 'You're the most honest person I've ever known.'

Matt laughed. 'That's not always a good thing! I think my honesty was what terrified you all those years ago, and admit it, it terrified you again when I was last here, didn't it?'

Fern had a sudden vision of herself dressed in Laura Ashley and living in a remote cottage where she dug up vegetables and delivered calves in her spare time. 'A little bit,' she admitted.

'A big bit, you fibber!' Matt said. 'I got carried away as always and it scared the hell out of you because, whatever it is that is between us, it still isn't quite enough to bridge the differences, is it?'

She swallowed. 'Maybe not.'

'And even if we chose to ignore those differences,' he continued, raising her hands to his lips and kissing them gently, 'it wouldn't be long before we were both unhappy and resenting one another. You'd be longing for the city and feeling tied down whereas I'd be miserable because I want to have children and dogs and the whole country lifestyle.'

'But I do want children one day!' Fern blurted. What! Where had that come from? She'd never really thought about having children, but then again she hadn't ruled out the possibility either.

'I'm sure you do and you'll be a fantastic mother,' Matt told her. 'I can picture them now wearing glittery clothes and making cakes smothered in hundreds and thousands. But search your heart, Fern, and deep down you already know that I'm not going to be the man you have them with, don't you?'

'Matt—' Fern tried to speak but her throat was too tight with sadness for words. Her gaze blurred and two tears rolled down her cheeks.

'Hey, don't cry.' Matt tenderly wiped each tear away with his thumb and then dropped a butterfly-soft kiss on her trembling lips. 'You shouldn't be sad, Fern. Don't you see? Our meeting again has been a good thing because it's answered all the what ifs that we always had about each other. I spent so long being bitter and angry and then wondering about what could have been that I probably spent more time in the past than I did in the present. How could I possibly move on with my life and commit myself to another woman if I was always obsessing about what could have been with you?'

Fern closed her eyes. She couldn't bear to look

into his warm ones because although he was so generous and so right part of her really wanted to change his mind. No matter what he said about their being incompatible, she'd still undervalued him.

'I should never have interfered in your life,' she whispered. 'I'm so sorry, Matt.'

'Don't be sorry!' Matt cupped her face in his hands and fixed Fern with a stern look. 'My God, Fern, don't you see? You've set us both free to move on with our lives. Yes, we wish it could have been different, but at least now we know the truth. No more regrets and no more maybes.'

She nodded. Wasn't this what she'd wanted? So none of her exes had turned out to be the love of her life, but at least now she knew and Matt was right: she could move on.

But quite where she'd move to she wasn't sure.

Suddenly Fern wanted to cry with the realisation of where she'd been going wrong all these years. Guys were attracted to her because she seemed to be such a free spirit while she, lacking roots, was always drawn to guys who *seemed* really solid. The men she chose had solid ambitions like Luke or secure finances like Matt or exciting careers like Seb; these were the qualities she'd sought, however unconsciously. Then, when she began to doubt her partners' reliability, she pulled away and felt disillusioned. Maybe it was time she stopped expecting the man in her life to be her foundation and started to feel more solid herself. Putting down roots by building her career was the way forward, rather than expecting her fairy-tale prince to step in and rescue her with marriage and family. This was the post-feminist era, after all. Weren't girls supposed to rescue themselves now?

'I'm in love with Amanda and I'm going to marry her,' Matt was saying. 'She's a good woman, Fern. Maybe she doesn't make my heart twist with joy like it does when I think of the times we spent together, but she's brave and strong and true and I know in my heart that she's absolutely one hundred per cent right for me. We're twin souls.'

'Amanda delivers calves,' Fern blurted.

What? Where the hell did that come from? It must be shock.

'Yes, she does.' Matt laughed. 'Which I don't think is a skill you'd have been keen to learn!'

Fern widened her eyes. 'Do I look like a girl who'd deliver calves?'

'Not in the slightest! But I bet you can apply your make-up while you drive!'

She held up her hands. 'Fair cop.'

'So you see, it would never have worked out, would it?'

Fern shook her head. 'I wish you and Amanda all the happiness in the world together.'

There. She really would get to heaven now!

'Thanks,' said Matt. Beads of perspiration sparkled on his forehead. 'Phew, I was really worried about saying all that. I've stressed about it for ages.'

'It's fine,' Fern said and to her surprise it really was. Yes, part of her was really sad, but it was sadness at letting go of a dream rather than at losing Matt. In fact when she thought of the narrow escape she'd had from living in Muckly under Bucket or wherever it was Matt wanted to relocate them to Fern actually felt like weeping tears of relief.

'So can we leave our relationship in the past and move on? Forget that any of this ever happened? I'd really appreciate it if I could tell Amanda about us in my own way,' Matt asked, a note of desperation in his voice. The word *please* hung in the air like the trail left by a sparkler on Bonfire Night.

Fern twisted a curl round her forefinger. 'Relax, Matt. I'm not about to come over and boil your hamsters. What's to tell Amanda anyway? Nothing really happened apart from you meeting up with an old girlfriend and realising what a lucky escape you'd had.'

'I'm so glad we've talked,' said Matt, his face breaking into a wide smile. 'I was really worried for a while that I'd given you the wrong idea and screwed everything up. You're a fantastic person but let's face it, we'd be hopeless together.'

Fern closed her eyes. The tsunami of emotions, from excited anticipation right through to rejection, that had overwhelmed her since he'd called had left her feeling shell-shocked. Of course Matt loved Amanda. He'd been blissfully happy until Fern had decided to rake over the past; he'd never been at ease with the idea of her reappearing in his life. Why ever would that have changed? How stupid had she been to think that Matt was coming over to fulfil the prophecy?

The answer was almost as stupid as she'd been to believe it all in the first place. Of course there was no prophecy. It had been nothing but smoke and mirrors, a good piece of entertainment for a girls' night in, and Fern had believed in it totally. As usual she'd thrown herself heart and soul into an idea without taking stock and weighing it up sensibly.

Would she never learn?

21

'Babes, are you really sure this is a good idea?' Zoe looked worried as she followed Fern across the Terminal Five concourse. 'This seems like a very sudden decision.'

'Those are always the best ones.' Fern craned her neck up at the departures board. 'My God, Zo, they're calling my flight. I'll have to go. Will you be able to take my car back and give the keys to Mum?'

'Of course,' said Zoe, trying to stuff Fern's enormous key ring, all fluffy toys and about two actual keys, into her Mulberry tote. 'And I'll water the house plants, and forward the mail and drop your letter of resignation in to Jeremy. You know I will. But do you really have to rush it? This is a huge decision to make overnight.'

But Fern wasn't listening; she was far too busy trundling the zebra-print case towards the departures lounge. Doubling her speed, Zoe caught her friend's patchwork jacket and pulled her round to face her.

'Fern! You're not getting on that plane until you tell me what all this is about,' she said firmly. There was a glint in her hazel eyes that meant business. 'One minute you want to live in London and be close to your family, the next you're uprooting yourself for a new life in the Czech Republic. It doesn't make sense.'

'You're absolutely right; none of it makes any sense.' Fern shook her head, her big earrings swaying in time with the movement. 'Look, Zoe, you'll probably think I'm crazy but this is just something I have to do. It's something for me. I've made a lot of mistakes lately and this is my way of putting them right. Don't look at me like that. I'm not running away or off after another hare-brained idea. I really want to take this job.'

Zoe frowned, and Fern noticed suddenly how pale and drawn her friend looked. That was another thing for Fern to feel bad about. She'd been so busy chasing down her prophecy over the weeks since the wedding that she'd hardly seen her best friend or even taken the time to call her that often. Zoe in turn had been really busy with work, and Fern had felt awkward about just turning up on the newly-weds. Well, that was another thing that was going to change now that she was over her search for the elusive one who'd got away. She'd make more time for her friends and family, fly them all out to Prague at her personal expense if she had to.

She waited for Zoe to say something, maybe give her a lecture about always jumping in feet first, but to Fern's amazement she just sighed. 'I'll really miss you,' she said sadly. 'It won't be the same without you.'

'Are you all right?' Fern asked, alarmed. Usually Zoe was the one *she* leaned on, the sensible one who'd dish out good advice like the school nurse dishing out cod liver oil. 'You look exhausted.'

Zoe shrugged her slim shoulders and gave Fern a smile which didn't quite reach her eyes. 'Oh, just ignore me. I'm being selfish. Prague will be fantastic for you. It's a brilliant opportunity.'

'Bugger Prague,' Fern said. 'What's wrong?' Then a thought occurred. 'You're not pregnant, are you?'

Zoe laughed. 'Stop trying to create a drama out of my life, Fern Moss, and concentrate on your own! No, just for the record I'm not pregnant, but I am absolutely shattered. Work's been totally hectic but that's a good thing really, isn't it? It's always good to be turning contracts down rather than fighting for them.'

'As long as you're fine.'

'I'm absolutely fine! And anyway, don't try to change the subject. I'm not the one running away to Prague, am I? Are you going to tell me what's going on?'

Fern hesitated. Zoe was such a thoughtful, careful person. From her crisp white shirt and 1940s-style trouser suit to her matching bag to her well-organised personal life, everything about her was measured and well planned. Zoe would never throw herself at random men just on a psychic's flimsy prediction, and neither would she run away to another country because she couldn't bear the failure of being left behind while everyone else moved on with their lives. No, Zoe would just square her shoulders and plot the best and most tested course. If Fern had been as pragmatic as her best friend who knows what might have happened.

'Things just got a bit weird,' she said slowly. 'I kind of got confused about some stuff.'

'Is this to do with what that psychic said at my hen night?' Zoe asked, as Fern handed her passport over to the check-in desk.

'Wow. Who's psychic now?'

'Don't look so surprised,' said Zoe, with a smile. 'I know you inside out, remember? It was the prophecy, wasn't it?'

'Maybe,' Fern admitted. 'Do you remember how she said I'd let the love of my life go? That I'd thrown away my soulmate?'

'Yes,' said Zoe slowly, her brow pleating with concern. 'And then we talked after the episode with Matt and agreed that you'd wait and see what unfolded.' She slapped her hand against her forehead. 'Duh! Except that this is you we're talking about, isn't it? You couldn't wait for anything; it would kill you. Oh God, Fern. Please tell me you didn't go tracking them all down?'

'Er, yes, I'm afraid so.' She scooped up her tickets and gave Zoe a rueful smile. 'I decided to give fate a helping hand so I traced them all and guess what? Surprise, surprise, it hasn't worked out with any of them.'

'No wonder you haven't called me for weeks. You didn't dare.'

Fern hung her head. 'Guilty, m'lud.'

'You know tracing them is *such* a bad idea?'

'I do now!' Fern said, slapping sticky labels on to her funky case and watching it trundle away to baggageland. 'You'd have told me to just wait and see, wouldn't you?'

'Too bloody right I would!' Zoe crossed her arms and gave Fern a stern look. 'It was all nonsense anyway, babes. Libby should have known better than to invite a psychic over just before a wedding. Not good timing.'

Fern looked up. 'You never did tell me what she said to you.'

'Nothing worth worrying about,' said Zoe quickly. 'Unlike you, I'm not one to grab fate by the short and curlies so I have no excitement to report. I'm an old married woman now, remember?'

'Being single's not all it's cracked up to be,' said Fern sadly. 'Come over and visit me, Zoe, and I'll tell you all about how Seb tried to propose and then added that he'd been seeing Vanessa all along, or how Luke Scottman decided we were better off in the past.'

Zoe's mouth hung open. Fern could almost see her breakfast. 'You saw Luke? For real? And Seb proposed? What the hell was he thinking?'

'He was thinking that I didn't care that he'd been seeing Vanessa for much longer than he'd let on. Like it didn't matter that it was a fully fledged affair rather than a quickie in the office. Wanker!'

'Wanker,' Zoe echoed, looking stunned.

'So, I'm giving up on them all and going to live in Prague,' declared Fern. 'Where I shall focus on my career and never think again about stupid prophecies.'

'You are so going to suffer for keeping all this from me. I'm supposed to be your best friend!' Zoe scolded. 'So those two didn't work out. That's hardly a surprise, is it? Surely you don't need to hide in Prague from them? Luke lives in LA and Seb rarely strays out of Richmond so you're pretty safe.'

Fern grinned. 'You left one out.'

'Not Matt?' Zoe looked horrified. 'Babes, he's engaged! I told you that at my wedding.'

'This is a call for BA flight 235 to Prague,' announced the tannoy. 'Will all passengers please present their boarding cards at gate seventeen.'

'It's a long story and I will tell you everything, I promise,' said Fern, hating the hurt expression on Zoe's face. 'I didn't say anything because I knew deep down I was being as bad as Vanessa, but I had to know for sure whether Matt was the one.' She took a deep breath. 'Last night I really thought he was coming round to tell me he loved me but instead he said he loved his fiancée and wanted me to back off. So I totally got that wrong, just like I always get it wrong! I'm such an idiot.'

Zoe shook her smooth blond head. 'You didn't get anything wrong, babes. None of those guys was right for you. I can't believe you ever believed they could be. What were you thinking?'

'I was thinking about how Angela said I'd let the love of my life go. Can you imagine how awful that feels?' Fern wailed. 'So it had to have been one of them and I couldn't risk getting it wrong. I did everything to try and put it right, Zo, everything that I could think of short of turning back time, and it still didn't work out. So, last night I just thought sod the prophecy and sod all the useless men, it's time to do something for me. That's why I've decided to take Alek up on his job offer and make a new start in Prague. After all, what have I got to lose?'

Zoe looked shocked. 'You've never mentioned any of this. I had no idea Angela's prophecy had upset you so much. I wish you'd told me.'

'Well, you've been pretty secretive about it all yourself,' Fern pointed out. 'Take it from me, though, Zoe: whatever Angela said to you it's a load of old bollocks.'

'I've never doubted that for a second.' Pausing at the entrance to the departures lounge, Zoe flung her arms round Fern and held her tight. 'Whatever happened, Fern, I still love you. None of it matters to your friends. We'd never judge you.'

Fern swallowed a sob. 'I love you too, Zoe. I wish I'd told you everything now.'

'You can invite me to Prague and tell me all about it there,' said Zoe firmly. 'I'm already looking forward to visiting. I'll leave Steve behind and we'll have a proper girls' weekend.'

'Sounds great,' Fern agreed, then nearly shot into orbit as her flight was called for the final time. 'Shit! I've got to go!'

'Take care, babes, won't you?' Zoe murmured into Fern's curls before letting her out of their embrace. 'And if Prague doesn't work out you know we're all here to look after you, okay?'

'Okay,' Fern gulped. Zoe was so tender-hearted that if she didn't get through that gate soon they'd both be howling. 'I'll call you when I'm sorted.'

'You'd better,' Zoe said. Her eyes were bright. 'Go on, then. You need to catch that plane.'

Fern took a deep breath. This really was it. She was leaving everything and everyone behind. Was she doing the right thing? Maybe she should just forget it all and go home with Zoe. But then Zoe lifted her hand to wave and the sharp planes of her engagement ring caught the light, sending emerald beams bouncing across the concourse floor. The symbolism couldn't have been clearer if a Greek chorus had strolled across the concourse and announced it. Zoe was married and settled; how could she possibly understand what life was like for Fern? Without her prophecy she was like an anchorless boat on a stormy sea. Of course moving on was the right decision. Hoisting her bag on to her shoulder and blowing Zoe one last kiss, Fern strode into Departures and didn't look back.

Her new life started here.

22

Dashing across Prague in a taxi was not anywhere near as romantic as the movies would have you believe. As Fern's driver negotiated his way through the afternoon traffic, cutting up Ladas and elegant Mercedes with equal determination, she closed her eyes, clung to the plastic seat and prayed that she'd make it to Alek's house in one piece. Perhaps it had been a big mistake to ask him to cross the city as quickly as possible. She hadn't come this far to end up a little blot of Fern jam on the main road from the airport.

No way, thought Fern with determination. This was the start of a new chapter in her life.

She'd debated whether or not to tell Alek that she was coming back. In the end she'd decided to just surprise him. It had seemed like a good idea at two a.m. but now, twelve hours later, Fern was starting to feel nervous. Perhaps she should have warned him first?

Finally, and against all the odds, Fern's taxi made it through the traffic and pulled up safely outside Alek and Francesca's house. Sending up a hasty prayer of thanks that she was still alive – at least the dash across Prague had proved that she wasn't suicidal yet – Fern collected her bags and handed the driver a fistful of crumpled korunas.

'See, I get you here quick, yes?' He grinned.

Fern's stomach was still in the arrivals lounge. 'Very quick,' she agreed. 'Please, keep the change.'

The cabbie beamed at Fern and then thrust a card into her hand, imploring her to use his services again. Either she'd totally overpaid him or nobody else in the Czech Republic was mad enough to use his services. As he zoomed off, waving cheerily, Fern took a deep breath. This was it. Time to see if Alek still wanted to employ her and whether she could make a go of life in Prague.

It was a sunny autumnal day with a fresh breeze sending clouds scudding across a Comfort blue sky. The air was sharper than at Heathrow, as though invigorated with new hope and excitement, and even the elegant trees that lined the street seemed a brighter and zestier green. Cheered by such a blatant display of symbolism, Fern felt her heart begin to dance.

She shrugged her rucksack up on to her shoulders and started to drag her case up the flight of marble steps which led to Alek's glossy blue door. By the time she reached the top she was puffing, and so engrossed in bumping the case on to the top step that she didn't notice Francesca hurtling out of the front door with an enormous box in her arms.

'Oh!' cried Francesca, catching her foot on Fern's suitcase and sprawling on to the step. 'My things!' She reached out her hands to try to break her fall but it was too late. Seconds later the box and all its belongings were rolling down the steps, followed by Fern's suitcase and then by Fern too.

'My God, Fern!' gasped Francesca. 'I'm so sorry! Are you okay? I didn't see you there. I thought you'd gone home?'

The world dipped and rolled for a second and the zebra-print wheelie case would never be the same again, but Fern was still in one piece.

'I'm fine,' she said, flexing her limbs just to make sure. 'And I did go home but I've decided to come back and take Alek up on his job offer, if he'll still have me.'

Francesca gave Fern a faint smile. 'I'm sure he'll be

delighted.' She pushed her long dark hair behind her ears and started to scoop up some of her belongings. 'He's always saying how talented and creative you are.'

'Is he?' Fern was relieved to hear it. 'That's good. To be honest I'll be stuffed if he doesn't want to employ me. I handed my notice in this morning.'

Chess shook her head. 'Fern, you're crazy!'

'Probably, but sometimes you don't have any choice but to do something dramatic,' Fern said with a shrug. 'I made some very hard decisions last night, but I'm pretty sure they're the right ones for me even if they were tough.'

'I understand.' Chess nodded. 'I'm in the same position myself.' She swept her hand in the direction of her scattered belongings. 'But you've probably already gathered that.'

'Are you having a clean-out?'

There were certainly a lot of belongings crammed into one box. Pictures of Alek and Chess drifted on to the street like photographic snowflakes, well-thumbed books had tumbled to the pavement and a large yucca plant sat drunkenly in its shattered pot. Now that she looked more closely Fern noticed that four black bin bags were already arranged neatly outside the front door, flanked by two calfskin suitcases and a stereo.

'Not exactly,' Chess said. 'I'm moving out.'

Fern's stomach lurched. 'Why? What's going on?'

Francesca sank on to one of the steps, drawing her knees up against her chest and wrapping her arms tightly round them. 'Isn't it obvious? I'm leaving Alek.'

'What? No!' Fern couldn't have been more shocked. 'You guys are great together!'

'Not any more, I'm afraid. Come on, Fern, you've been staying with us. You must have seen how things were.'

Fern thought back. The tension between Alek and Chess had been apparent the evening Tomas and Eliska had come over for dinner, and Alek had said himself he was afraid that they wanted different things. Then there was the night when Alek had left the engagement party to rescue Fern and had shown little inclination to go rushing back. Chess was right; the clues *were* there if you looked closely.

It was just as well that Fern had chosen set design as a career. She'd have made a rubbish detective.

'Alek and I want different things,' Chess said quietly, echoing Fern's thoughts. 'He's happy living in the city or travelling around to different locations at the drop of a hat. He loves never knowing what's going to happen from one day to the next, or having to change his plans at a moment's notice.'

Fern said nothing. She totally understood where Alek was coming from.

'But I don't want to live like that any more,' Francesca continued. 'It's the right time for me to move on with my life and I think that in order to do that I have to accept that Alek and I are just too different to make it work. One of us might be happy but it would absolutely be at the expense of the other.'

'I totally understand.' Fern closed her eyes and saw Matt again as he told her his dream of a country lifestyle. 'I had a boyfriend who wanted to move to the countryside and keep chickens. I'd rather chew my arm off than be more than five minutes from Starbucks but it was his idea of heaven. We'd have made each other miserable.'

'What happened?' asked Chess, her brown eyes wide.

'He found someone who was perfect for him,' Fern said, and as she said it she knew it was one hundred per cent true. 'They've bought a cottage in the sticks and chickens and everything.'

Francesca frowned. 'What is this sticks?'

'It means the middle of nowhere? The country-side? Anyway, forget that. All that matters is that they had a dream that matched whereas he and I didn't. The only chicken I want to handle comes from KFC.'

Chess bit her lip. 'It is the same for us, I think? Alek and I don't match. Seeing you two together last week, chatting about work and joking together, really showed me how far apart we'd grown.'

Fern was horrified. 'Chess, there's nothing going on between me and Alek, if that's the problem! Honestly! Please don't think that! Alek isn't the reason I'm back!'

Francesca touched Fern gently on the arm. Her eyes shone like wet peat. 'What I'm saying is that I've realised it's time to move on. It's sad, but these things happen. Maybe now we will both be free to find our perfect match?'

Feeling choked at this but unable to argue against such faultless logic all Fern could do was give Chess a hug before helping her to load her belongings into her smart red BMW. Once Chess had driven away with her first carload Fern headed into the house. Her first thought was for Alek. He adored Francesca – he'd left family and friends in London to follow her back to Prague – and she knew he'd be really upset.

She just hoped it wasn't her presence in the house that had driven the final wedge between them. Chess had made a good point; when Alek and Fern started talking shop they were more BlueWater than the local Spar and hours could pass in a flash for them while everyone else died of boredom. *Surely I can't have messed up another male friendship*, Fern thought bleakly as she abandoned her suitcase in the cool hallway. *That would have to be some kind of record.*

The house was still, as though holding its breath. The hallway was as immaculate as always, the old grandfather clock tick tocking away the minutes from the foot of the stairs and the large antique chandelier scattering sunshine diamonds across the chequered floor. Alek's leather satchel was looped over the bottom of the banister and his black leather coat hung on the peg by the kitchen door. He was in then, sitting somewhere quietly while Francesca dismantled the pieces of their life together. He wouldn't be able to bear watching her collect her belongings. Fern knew that he hated saying goodbye and always chose to absent himself. He felt things deeply and unlike Fern, who dealt with high emotion by creating a drama, Alek always chose to find a quiet space. It didn't mean he felt things less, Fern had come to realise; it just meant he dealt with them differently.

As she crossed the hall, shrugging off her fake fur jacket, she felt really nervous. She'd only been gone twenty-four hours but already the world had shifted on its axis. It felt as though she'd last seen Alek lifetimes ago. In many ways it had been a lifetime ago. When she'd left Prague she'd been full of high hopes that her prophecy was only hours way from being fulfilled. As her cab zoomed through the elegant tree-lined boulevards of the city en route to the airport her stomach had flip-flopped with the delicious anticipation that she might soon be reunited with Matt. She'd imagined a life of being his partner and planning weddings; she'd even imagined the chubby-cheeked children with Matt's dark eyes and her blond curls . . .

She shook her head impatiently as though to shake off the images. What a total bloody idiot she'd been. None of it was real. That life had only existed inside her heated imagination. Now she was back as a single woman, homeless and jobless and about to throw herself on Alek's hospitality. It probably couldn't have come at a worse time for him.

'Hello,' she called. 'Alek? It's me, Fern. Where are you?'

'Fern?' She heard a chair scrape the stone floor in the kitchen followed by his light tread across the floor. Then Alek appeared in the doorway, his tie undone and a glass of Scotch clasped in one slender artistic hand. His dark eyes were bruised by purple smudges, his jaw was shadowed with stubble, and beneath the swarthy complexion he looked pale, the skin across his sculpted cheekbones taut with emotion. His eyes widened in surprise when he saw Fern standing in the hall. 'My God, it really is you. What are you doing here?'

'Never mind me right now. None of my stuff's important. Are *you* okay?'

Alek shrugged. 'I take it you bumped into Chess then?' He sighed. 'I'm not going to lie and say it's come as a shock, but it hasn't been very pleasant. And I never realised she owned all the cushions. What is it with girls and cushions?'

Alek looked so bleak as he said this that Fern's heart went out to him. Flying across the hall she flung her arms round her friend and hugged him tightly. 'I've got hundreds too; it's definitely a girl thing. Don't worry; I'll donate them all to you.'

In spite of the sadness etched on to his face Alek laughed. 'I bet they're all pink and fluffy or leopard print, yes?'

She punched him playfully on the arm. 'There's nothing wrong with that. If you're really lucky I may lend you the one with mirrors I've had since university. What do you think?'

Alek looked down at his half-empty glass. 'I think

I need another drink. Do you want one?'

From the hallway the grandfather clock struck half past one. 'Go on then. The sun's over the yard arm, as my mother always says,' Fern agreed, following Alek into the kitchen and perching on one of the painfully trendy stools that flanked the granite work surface.

'I don't know why you're here,' said Alek as he poured her a generous measure into a sparkling crystal glass, 'but I'm bloody glad to see you.'

Fern laid her hand on his. 'I'm so sorry my timing's crap, Al. I'd never have landed myself on you if I'd known all this was going on.'

He shook his dark head. 'I'm glad to see a friendly face. It's been like a new cold war here. You must have noticed how things were while you were staying? Things were a little chilly between Chess and me.'

She bit her lip. Glacial might have described it better after the dinner party. 'Alek, it wasn't my being here that made things difficult between you, was it? You know what they say about house guests and the three day rule?'

He looked confused. 'Is that some strange English saying?'

'Yeah, I think it must be. It's another of Cybil's gems.' Fern swirled the amber liquid thoughtfully.

'It means that guests are like fish – get rid of them after three days.'

'That's funny!' Alek threw back his head and laughed. Fern noticed how strong his throat was as the muscles contracted and rippled. Then he sighed and laid his hand on hers. 'It's funny, but not true in your case, Fern. Chess and I splitting up has nothing to do with your staying here, I promise. We'd just come to the end of the road. Remember how I told you that we wanted different things?'

Fern nodded. 'You said it was causing problems between you.'

'It certainly was.' Alek watched her closely, his head slightly tilted as though considering what to say next. 'Listen, Fern, don't take it the wrong way but maybe having you here highlighted just how little Chess and I have in common these days. It was good for me to be able to discuss my work without feeling guilty or boring someone half to death.' He passed a hand over his eyes. 'I think we both realised we'd gone as far as we could. It was time to part.'

'But it's so sad!'

'But the right thing for us both,' said Alek softly. 'We need to move on. There are some things that just aren't meant to be.'

'Just like me and Matt,' Fern told him sadly. 'That didn't work out either. We're too different to ever make a future together.'

Alek sloshed some more whisky into her glass. 'What a great pair we make, eh?'

They sat next to each other sipping their drinks in companionable silence for a while.

'About us making a good pair,' Fern said eventually. 'That's kind of the reason I came back. I was wondering . . . no, actually I'm more than wondering, I'm really hoping, that you meant what you said about me coming to work for you?'

Alek stared at her. His drink hovered halfway between the counter and his lips.

'I mean, if that's okay?' Fern added quickly. 'I mean, if it isn't that's fine. I wouldn't want to intrude or anything.'

Maybe now wasn't the best time to tell him she'd quit her job and flown back to Prague on a hunch that it was the right thing to do. It was probably best that a potential new boss didn't think she was a total flake, even though most of her friends thought you could stick her in a 99 ice cream and not be able to tell the difference.

'Fern Moss,' said Alek, and now his eyes shone like treacle. 'You've gone and handed in your notice, haven't you!?' He slammed his drink down and took her hands in his. 'You've really done it!'

It was a bit disconcerting that her potential new business partner knew her so well, thought Fern. But then he always had been able to read her like a book, albeit one with a platform-booted fluffy cover.

'Does your offer still stand?' she asked. 'Do you still want to work with me? Maybe friends shouldn't work together?'

'Of course they bloody well should!' Alek cried, a smile of such sudden sweetness splitting his face that Fern almost kissed him. 'And of course the job offer still stands. Haven't I been trying to persuade you to move here for the last year?' He jumped to his feet and began to rummage in the wine rack. 'I think we need some champagne to toast this new business partnership! We'll make the best team. We always did, didn't we?'

'We certainly did,' Fern agreed. 'We never stopped laughing, either.' She started to giggle at a memory. 'Do you remember when we did the set for the Camelot show?'

'And you ended up locking yourself in the pretend chastity belt?' Alek chuckled, pulling a bottle of Cristal from the fridge. 'How could I forget that? The props guys were really annoyed when it had to be cut off.'

Fern pulled a mock indignant face. 'Er, can I just remind you who dared me a drink if I put it on?'

Laughing and sharing memories they grew more nostalgic by the second, and with every memory the smarting pain about getting the prophecy so wrong began to lessen. Even the recollection of closing the door on a future with Matt had somehow lost its sting. Fern only hoped that Alek was feeling the same about Chess. He was such a good friend that she would have liked nothing more than to soothe away his heartache too. Perhaps working together would help them both to move on.

Alek popped the cork and poured Fern a brimming flute of champagne.

'To a long and successful partnership,' he said as he raised his glass, 'and to old friends making a new start.'

Fern clinked her glass against his, her spirits rising and fizzing just like the bubbles. There'd be no more dwelling in the past or wasting her time with silly prophecies. This was a new start and a whole new life.

She could hardly wait to begin!

23

'And cut!' the director called. 'Good job, everyone. That's it for the night.'

There was a collective sigh of relief from the crew. The director of *Nauticus*, the latest swash-buckling Luke Scottman vehicle, was notoriously demanding and it wasn't unusual for his shoots to overrun by several hours. Fern didn't usually mind but this was a night shoot on a Cornish cliff top, it was gone midnight, the air was glacial, she was shivering inside her thick down jacket and even her goose bumps had goose bumps. Christ only knew how Luke must be feeling in his thin linen shirt and breeches.

'Thank God!' Alek said, smothering a yawn. 'I thought he'd never be satisfied with any of those takes.'

'If I'd had to tweak that candlelit seduction set

one more time I think I'd have screamed,' Fern moaned, blowing on her fingertips and stamping her numb feet. 'Talk about a perfectionist.'

'He's one of the top directors in the world, though, and it won't do our reputation any harm to have worked with him,' Alek reminded her with a proud smile.

'Mmm, so maybe NOMO Set Design is a victim of its own success?' said Fern, whose idea of fun certainly wasn't freezing to death at one a.m. 'Next time I don't care how brilliant a film is or what a great contract it is for our company, if the director's a sadist we're saying no.'

In the three months since Alek and Fern had started their set design company they'd been inundated with work and were building an impressive name in the industry. Winning the tender for designing the set for this new historical film, a kind of Cornish smugglers meets *Pirates of the Caribbean*, had been the icing on the cake, and they'd been so busy either designing or away on location that Fern's feet had hardly touched the ground. She hadn't even had time to sort out her own flat yet so she was still renting a room at Alek's and the arrangement worked surprisingly well. They never rowed, Fern got to eat Alek's amazing cuisine and in return she'd transformed his rather austere and minimalist house into a riot of textures and colours and even managed to stop Alek being too maudlin about breaking up with Chess. Actually, thought Fern, as she swiftly packed away the set, he'd also done a wonderful job of taking her mind off the entire prophecy fiasco. In fact life in Prague was everything she had hoped for and more. Creatively she'd never been more fulfilled – working with Alek really inspired her – and her social life was so busy that sometimes whole weeks passed without a night in.

'All done?' Alek asked when he returned from loading up a handcart with props.

Fern nodded. 'It certainly is, thank God. What's the time?'

Alek shrugged and she noticed a pale gap on his wrist where his Rolex usually had pride of place. 'One o'clock maybe? It's certainly late.'

'You're not kidding,' Fern agreed. If she didn't find a bed soon she'd fall asleep right here on the damp grass. 'Can we please go now? I'm desperate to have a hot drink and crash out.'

'What? You don't want to go and party with the crew? You must be getting old!' he teased.

Fern couldn't think of anything worse. All she wanted to do was thaw out and then sleep for hours.

'You go ahead,' she told Alek. 'I'll just check in at the hotel and catch you guys in the morning.'

'Ah. There's a slight problem with that.' Alek couldn't have looked more sheepish if he'd grown a fleece and started bleating. 'About the hotel—'

'I know that look,' said Fern, putting her hands on her hips and pulling a mock stern face. 'That's your "I've forgotten to do it" face, last seen a few weeks ago when you were on location in Venice and forgot your mother's birthday. Didn't you have to send someone very kind, and not too far from here, out to choose her a present and buy her lunch?'

He held up his hands. 'Guilty! Anyway, apparently there's only one tiny hotel in the village and it was fully booked weeks ago. Ditto every guest house. I'm really sorry.'

'Oh, Alek! Not another night camping in the van? We'll die of hypothermia.'

'Would I do that to you?' Alek asked. Then he thought about it. 'Okay, yes, maybe I would but not tonight. When I found that everywhere was full I used my initiative, and a pretty major bribe, to secure comfortable accommodation for the night.' He raised his wrist and rolled his dark eyes.

'Not your watch!' Fern gasped. 'Oh, Al, you didn't

have to do that. I know what that watch means to you.'

'It means more that I don't let you down. I dragged you out on this job so the least I owe you is a comfortable bed for the night.'

'I can hardly wait!' Fern said, taking his arm as they zigzagged down the steep cliff path towards the dark village. 'It must be pretty special if it cost you a Rolex. I think I know exactly the place. Does it have a view of the sea?' On the way into the small fishing village she'd noticed an imposing grey stone house overlooking the jelly-green water. How amazing would it be to stay there in a stately four-poster, all wrapped up in a goose-feather eiderdown, and wake up to a view of the sparkling waves.

'There's certainly a guaranteed sea view,' Alek promised her. 'And I think it will definitely be a once-in-a-lifetime experience.'

The cliff path widened into a cobbled street which came to an abrupt halt at the harbour wall where trawlers rode the tide, groaning at their moorings as the waves slapped against their hulls.

'Here we are,' said Alek proudly.

Fern was confused and a bit annoyed. 'Al, what are we doing practically on the beach?'

'See that boat there?' He pointed across the

harbour to a small yacht bobbing merrily on the rising tide.

She squinted in the general direction. '*Dawn Raider*?'

'That's right,' Alek said, starting to descend a rickety ladder that plunged dangerously into the inky water. 'That's where we're staying. It belongs to a local man I met in the pub at lunchtime. I managed to persuade him to loan it to me for the night. Luckily for us he agreed!'

Fern started to laugh. 'Of course he agreed, you muppet! A Rolex in exchange for a night on a boat? He must be delighted.'

'Well, yes,' Alek admitted. 'But this will be the sort of fun you can't put a price on. Come on,' he added as she dithered on the edge of the quay. 'Hurry up! What's the matter?'

'Al, I know it's never come up before but I'm not mad about sailing boats. I get seasick just looking at the *Blue Peter* logo!'

'You'll be fine, just follow me,' Alek called up. 'Come on, I won't let you fall. Trust me.'

'I do trust you,' muttered Fern as she wobbled after him. 'I'm just not sure I trust this ladder!'

At the foot of the ladder was a rowing boat so leaky it made the *Titanic* look watertight. Fern closed her eyes and prayed. Then she felt Alek's strong hands circle her waist as he swung her into the boat, which dipped and rolled horribly, and then they were off.

'You can open your eyes now,' chuckled Alek. He was kneeling precariously on the prow of the boat and guiding it by weaving the oar back and forth, darting between the other small vessels that were moored in the harbour.

'You never said you could row,' said Fern, impressed.

'You never asked. How else do you think I have this rippling physique? Designing sets?'

'Can't say I've noticed the rippling physique, but I'll take your word for it.'

Abruptly the boat bumped against the hull of the yacht.

'Home at last!' cried Alek.

He tied a complicated knot, heaved Fern up another ladder, dragged her across a skiddy deck and only just saved her from hurtling head first into the cabin. Inside it was surprisingly warm and Alek fiddled with a hurricane lamp that eventually illuminated the small space. Fern looked around. There were two narrow bunks, a teeny table and a sink so tiny that it looked like a bird bath. In the corner were a camping stove and a bucket.

'I'm guessing that's the lavatory,' said Alek, following her gaze.

'Fan-flipping-tastic,' said Fern.

'Don't say I don't take you to all the best places!'

'I won't say, don't worry!' she shot back, but when she noticed the worried expression on his face the bucket loo didn't seem to matter any more, not when Alek had tried so hard to please, and she smiled at him. 'Actually, it's really cosy and I love the sound of the waves and the tinkle of the rigging. I'll be fast asleep in no time.'

Alek's face softened with relief and closing the small door he shut out the inky night. Shadows pooled around the cabin, leaping and dancing as the wind kissed the flame in the lamp. This was a world away from Alek's beautiful house in Prague, yet there was something really peaceful about being stranded out on the water and the way that the waves rocked the little yacht made Fern's eyes even heavier.

Alek placed a gentle hand on her shoulder and guided her to a bunk. 'Why don't you sit down? I'm going to see if I can find something to drink. Apparently there's some champagne somewhere.'

Fern collapsed on to one of the bunks. It was so

narrow that Kate Moss would have barely fitted.

'Aha!' Alex plucked a bottle of Moët out of a minute fridge. 'Things are looking up!'

With a loud pop the cork flew out of the bottle. Amber liquid hissed over Alek's strong tanned hand as he poured two brimming mugfuls.

'I propose a toast,' he said, his slanting brown eyes sparkling. In the half-light of the cabin his teeth gleamed very white and Fern was taken aback to find herself thinking just how attractive he was; if you weren't his best friend, obviously.

'You and me, the best set designers in the business. To NOMO!'

They clashed their mugs together.

'We make a good team,' Fern said, after knocking back a serious amount of the sharp biscuity liquid. 'You were right; we should have gone into partnership years ago. Remember when we worked for Jeremy? We never stopped laughing.'

'We had a lot of fun,' said Alek, squeezing next to her on the bunk. 'I was devastated when I left to move to Prague. That was a bad day for me.'

Fern stared down at the table. It hadn't been a bad day just for him.

His supple fingers reached out to raise her chin so that she couldn't avoid his melting brown gaze.

'Do you still remember it?' he asked softly. 'Do you remember the day you let me go?'

Fern almost dropped her mug as Alek's choice of words resonated through every fibre. Of course she remembered that day. She remembered it perfectly. She and Alek had been halfway through a major project, working day and night to perfect a Victorian set for a bloodfest about vampires and strumpets, when he'd been offered the job in the Prague office. It had been the opportunity of a lifetime for Alek, and when he'd asked Fern whether she thought he should take it she'd put her personal feelings aside and told him to accept.

'You really think I should go?' Alek had asked, looking taken aback. 'But we're only halfway through this job.'

Biting back a rising sense of panic at the thought of losing her right-hand man Fern had pasted a bright smile on to her face. 'Sure,' she'd said, pretending to be absorbed by winding black lace round a dismembered dressmaker's mannequin. 'You're always saying how much Chess wants you to move there and spend more time with her. And Prague's your dream location, isn't it?'

But Alek had looked confused and more than a little put out. 'Won't it make things really hard for you if I go? I'd leave you right in the middle of the project.'

'Al,' Fern had said, 'I'll cope.'

'It wouldn't be fair. No,' he'd said with a small shake of his dark head. 'I won't go. There'll be other jobs. I won't let you down.'

Fern had been bowled over by Alek's loyalty to her but there was no way she was going to let him miss out on such a brilliant opportunity, especially if it meant he could be with Chess. In the end she'd practically had to order him to take the Prague job.

'Alek, for God's sake! I can't believe you're even thinking about turning this job down! What's to stay for?'

He'd stared back at her. 'I don't know, Fern. You tell me. What is there to stay for?'

Her eyes had slid away from his like butter from a warm knife. 'Nothing, Alek. Your life is moving on. You'd be crazy not to take the job. In fact, I insist you take it. If you don't I'll sack you!'

'Do you mean that?' Alek had sounded incredulous. 'You'd really let me go?'

Fern had swallowed the golf ball that someone had suddenly driven into her throat and turned to face him.

'Absolutely,' she'd said firmly. 'Of course I would.'

And that had been that. She'd let her closest friend and dearest colleague go for his own sake. It didn't matter that when he'd gone home she'd cried until she'd looked like a goblin or that at his leaving do she'd been in pieces. No one ever said that doing the right thing was easy, did they? Alek too had seemed strangely reluctant to say goodbye, but then Fern supposed that he was leaving everything behind to start again which was a pretty daunting prospect. They'd parted on good terms and as Alek's career in Prague went from strength to strength she'd felt proud that she'd been unselfish enough to release him from his contract.

But to be sitting with him now, closer than spoons in the tiny cabin, with the sea gently slapping the hull, and to hear Alek remind her that she'd *let him go* came as the most enormous shock. Every word in her vocabulary fell down in a dead faint and she just stared at him, unable to speak. Something was clicking and turning in her mind as the final pieces of celestial Tetris slotted into place.

'Can you say that again?' she whispered eventually.

In the buttery lamplight Alek's expression was masked by shadows. 'What? About wondering if you remembered the day you let me go?'

Fern felt the breath leave her body as though a Sumo wrestler had just landed on her solar plexus. It was so glaringly obvious that she almost laughed out loud. How could she have been so stupid?

'I let you go,' she whispered, the silence swelling as the sea strained to listen over the drumming of her heart. 'My God, it was you all along! Alek, you're the one I let go!'

Suddenly everything made perfect sense. It was as though she'd spent ages staring at the wrong side of a tapestry only to turn it over and discover that all the knots and tangled stitches were there for a deeper purpose. Even the time she'd spent with other guys fitted into the overall pattern. You can love many people in your lifetime, Fern realised, and for many different reasons, but you only had one soulmate. The tricky bit was figuring out who he was and holding on to him.

She stared at Alek as though seeing him for the very first time. All those weeks she'd wasted trying to figure it all out. She'd loved Matt and Seb and Luke in different ways but she'd always had to work at being the person she thought they wanted her to be. That's why those relationships never worked out – she'd been with the wrong guy!

The answer was, Fern realised suddenly, to be

with the person you can be most yourself around. And for her Alek was that person. He'd never been embarrassed by her or reprimanded her for her crazy dramatics; in fact more often than not he'd been her partner in crime and encouraged her. Take moving to Prague, for instance. Zoe and her family had been worried whereas Alek hadn't batted an eyelid.

Alek totally got her.

He always had.

'Are you okay?' Alek asked in alarm as Fern gaped at him. 'What's the matter? Are you ill? Say something, Fern. You've gone so white!' His strong arms tightened round her and he held her against his chest, smoothing her hair back from her pale face and whispering endearments in Czech. She gazed back at him, her heart skittering when she saw the love and concern in his treacle-dark eyes. Why hadn't she seen it before?

His hands either side of her face, Alek stared down at her. 'What's wrong? Please tell me, Fern. You know you can tell me anything.'

Her stomach lurched. Could she? Maybe there was only one way to find out?

'Alek,' she said shakily, 'there's something you need to know, something that I have to tell you.

Something I've known for ever deep down and that you tried to tell me a very long time ago. But I've been so stupid that I couldn't see what was right in front of me.'

Alek's eyes searched hers as though trying to read what she was saying. 'And what exactly is that something?' he asked softly.

Fern gulped. His face was so close to hers that his full soft lips were only a kiss away.

'Something I should have done a long time ago. Let me show you,' she whispered, and leaning forward she did the bravest thing she'd ever done in her life. She kissed Alek.

'Oh, Fern,' he groaned, his arms slipping round her shoulders as he pulled her so close that she could feel his heart galloping beneath the soft fabric of his shirt. 'Have you any idea how long I've been imagining us doing that?'

'Not really,' she whispered.

Alek traced the curve of her cheek with his forefinger. 'All my life,' he said softly and then he was kissing her again and nothing else mattered any more because all Fern could think about was that she never wanted the kiss to end and her insides melted like ice cream with the deliciousness of it. She loved the way his stubble rasped against her cheeks and the way that his lips seemed custom made to fit hers. Nothing else was important. And as they kissed the little boat rocked them gently on the turning tide, each wave in rhythm with the beating of their hearts.

Finally, as they broke apart smiling shyly at one another, Alek running his hands over her face as though to convince himself he wasn't dreaming, Fern realised she no longer needed a psychic to foresee her future. Her future, her past and her present was right here right now, holding her in his arms.

And now she'd found him Fern knew she was never letting go again.

You can buy any of these other
Little Black Dress titles from your
bookshop or *direct from the publisher*.

FREE P&P AND UK DELIVERY
(Overseas and Ireland £3.50 per book)

TO ORDER SIMPLY CALL THIS NUMBER

01235 400 414

or visit our website: www.headline.co.uk

Prices and availability subject to change without notice.